CLUES

ACROSS

17. Kill
25. Around a priest's neck
33. Comforter filling

DOWN

25. Jack ___ Jill

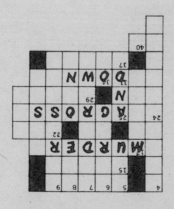

MURDER ACROSS AND DOWN

Herbert Resnicow

Puzzles by Henry Hook

BALLANTINE BOOKS • NEW YORK

Library of Congress Catalog Card Number: 84-91800

ISBN 0-345-32282-7

Manufactured in the United States of America

First Edition: June 1985

To Professor Edward Engelberg of Brandeis University, who was my first critic and has been of inestimable help since.

 **1**

'PARIS REJECTS CROSS-BONED FISH.' "I REALLY NEED
help," pleaded Janos Miklosz, as he studied the clue. "Six
letters, third letter *I*."

The seven directors were seated in the corner of The
Cruciverbal Club lounge. "If it's Paris from the Trojan
War," Delmore Rankin said, fussing with his paisley as-
cot, "I'm stumped. But if it's the city, there has to be a
French connection. 'Seines,' maybe? The river that runs
through Paris and is also a net for catching fish? But I
don't see that in the clue."

"I don't have enough trouble with English?" Janos
asked. "Now I have to contend with cryptic clues in
French?"

"Stop bitching, Janny," Vergil Yount drawled, taking
a long pull at his bourbon. "If everybody in New York
had as much trouble with languages as you Magyars, we
wouldn't need remedial reading in graduate school."

"Paris was the son of Priam," stated Norbert Kantor,
pushing his yarmulke back into place, "and that has third
letter *I*, so it might mean 'Pri's son,' which becomes
'prison.' The 'cross-boned fish' could be the poor fish
who is behind bars. Or is it possibly 'primal'? Maybe

1

there's a prehistoric fish with bones in the shape of a cross. The whiting has bones with a triradial cross-section."

"I'll bet that puzzle is by Hannibal," Caroline Trimble whispered, looking around nervously. "He's always so mean, doesn't obey the rules at all. I hate him."

"It is by Hannibal," said Miklosz, sweeping the black hair off his forehead. "That's why I'm doing it. Practicing for the big contest."

"Surely, my dear lady," Yount said, "you don't really hate anyone. You're much too nice for that."

"I do too," Caroline whispered. "Hannibal is dishonest. He's worse than the monsters who tear pages out of my books."

"Everybody stuck?" Lila Quinn peered at the group through her harlequin glasses. No one responded. "How about you, Brundage?"

Harvey Brundage smiled coldly. "I'm not in the habit of helping rivals," he said.

"Which means that creepy Harvey is stuck too." Lila Quinn ran her hand over her metallic-blond bouffant. "Okay. It's 'poison.' My Irwin, may he rest in peace, always pronounced it wrong when we went out to fancy places, which wasn't too often, I'm sorry to say."

"Another lucky guess, Lila," Norbert Kantor asked, "or deep analysis?"

"I don't analyze," Lila said, "and I *never* guess. I *know*. Besides, we're under the sign of Pisces today, so it's double positive."

"Lila strikes again," Janos said. "I see it now. Fish, in French is *poisson*. 'Rejects' is 'reject-s,' or, leave out the *s*. 'Cross-boned' is from 'skull and crossbones,' which stands for poison. Simple, once it's broken."

"That's what I mean," Caroline Trimble whispered in-

2

dignantly. "Hannibal cheated twice in one clue. You're not allowed to split directives the way he did with 'rejects,' and you have to give an *exact* definition in your clue, which Hannibal certainly didn't do. I'd like to poison *him*."

"I wondered about that name," Delmore Rankin said, removing his wire-rimmed glasses. "He didn't pick that title from the world of crosswords. Most constructors use names implying torture, such as Torquemada or Ximenes."

"I've figured that one out," said Norbert Kantor, stroking his Vandyke. "Hannibal was the name of the first crossword constructor."

"You've really flipped this time, Kantor." Harvey Brundage sneered. "Hannibal never constructed a crossword in his life. The first crossword was a word square from A.D. 300, five hundred years after Hannibal's death."

"I get it." Vergil Yount's fat face spread in a grin. "Hannibal crossed the Alps with elephants. Not bad for a Yankee."

"The screaming question is"—Delmore Rankin had a mischievous choir-boy smile on his beautiful face—"what do you get if you cross an Alp with an elephant?"

"There's an anagram there for sure." Vergil Yount began scribbling in his notebook.

"I'm sure there is," Kantor said. "What I had in mind—and I've been waiting for an opening for a week—is a riddle: What do you get when you cross the Alps with an elephant?"

"Elephant skis?" Lila asked.

"Close," Kantor admitted, "and not too bad. But my answer is more complex." There was a moment's silence while everyone thought. "Elephant wheelchairs," Kantor said triumphantly. Another moment's silence. "Because

3

when you cross the Alps with an elephant, you get defeated by the Romans." He smiled, satisfied, as everyone groaned.

"Let's not wait anymore for Sullivan." Harvey Brundage changed the subject, clearly unwilling to let Kantor enjoy his victory. "Let's get the meeting started. I've got some heavy practicing to do."

"Pretty smart of you to get born to a rich father, Harvey," Lila Quinn said sweetly, "so you could afford to practice ten hours a day. Poor stupid us, we all have to work for a living."

Brundage flushed. "It isn't all luck, you know. Brundage and Son tripled its dollar volume in the ten years since I became president."

"That took a lot of brains to accomplish in the arbitraging trade," said Janos Miklosz, "when inflation in that period quadrupled and gold hit eight hundred dollars an ounce."

"Arbitraging is a profession," Harvey said stiffly, "not a trade. And you're all jealous. And I'm glad you are. You can all spend the next week figuring out how to explain to your creditors that you can't pay your bills because stupid Harvey Brundage won *both* the solvers and the constructors contests. For the first time in the history of the club, to boot."

Giles Sullivan walked in just in time. "Now, children," he said, jauntily swinging his gold-headed cane, "enough bickering. I apologize for being so late. Somehow I find myself involved in more projects after retirement than when I was a working lawyer."

"All right," Miklosz said, "let's go into the conference room. But I'll go crazy if I don't have a cigarette first. Take a five-minute break while I go outside and smoke."

"I thought you were trying to quit," Caroline said.

"I am definitely quitting," he said, screwing a cigarette into his long ivory holder. "Right now. I just want to finish this pack."

 2

BEFORE GILES SULLIVAN COULD STOP HIM, MIKLOSZ picked up the gold-headed cane. "This is *heavy*," Miklosz said. "What's it made of, solid lead?"

"It has a steel center," Sullivan said. "I'm heavier than I look and sometimes I put my whole weight on it."

Miklosz tapped the cane lightly on the floor and said, "I hereby call this meeting of the board of directors of the Cruciverbal Club to order." Gone was the joking tone of the past half hour; this was Miklosz the businessman. "This ad hoc meeting has one item on the agenda: the final preparations for our great fiftieth-anniversary contests. Professor Kantor will report on the finances."

Norbert Kantor didn't need notes. "Raising the entry fee to one hundred dollars for the solvers contest and five hundred for the constructors contest had no effect on the number of entrants," Norbert Kantor stated. "They know how much harder it is to construct a puzzle than to solve one. Almost every member of the club is trying his luck."

"That's what I told you," Lila Quinn said complacently. "First prize of twenty-five thousand dollars is good odds."

"Not everybody is as money-hungry as you are, Lila,"

Harvey Brundage said. "Some of us are true amateurs; we're in it for love."

"You don't know what love is, creep," she replied. "You picked crosswords because you figured it's the best place for a wimp to become a champ fast. Well, in five years, with all your money and your tutors and your computers, you're still number nineteen in the club."

Harvey Brundage scowled. "This year will be different. I'm going to win in both categories; it's absolutely certain. And do you know what I'm going to do with the money? Piss it away, that's what. And you can eat your heart out, Lila, while you're hustling suckers in your penny-ante Scrabble games. Rankin can do the same while he's hanging around rich old fags, and Kantor's wife puts patches on his kids' patches, and—"

"That's enough, Brundage," Giles Sullivan barked in his courtroom voice, his light blue eyes no longer mild. "You will act like a gentleman in this club, or you will leave at once. I will see to it personally, if required." The tall spare gentleman looked directly into Brundage's eyes. Brundage mumbled a few words and looked down.

After a moment Norbert Kantor continued. "Since the publishers are putting up the prize money, we will have enough left to endow a scholarship in philology and to subsidize one book a year in the field."

"This is crazy," Brundage said. "We never agreed to that. The money should be used to reduce our dues."

"Then all of the wrong kinds of people could get in," Delmore Rankin said sweetly.

"You're right for once," Harvey said. "Then let's spruce up the place a bit; it's too dark and gloomy. We need a bigger bar and all that."

"This was Cornelius van Broek's home," Giles Sullivan said, "and it's quite luxurious as it is. As executor and

7

administrator of the estate, I see no need for improvement at this time. Why not move to use the profits from our semicentennial celebration to endow the scholarship and the publication?"

"So move," said Vergil Yount quickly.

"Second," whispered Caroline Trimble.

"Can't you see," Brundage said, "that Kantor is just trying to get more students for his classes so he can keep his job? And get his books published?"

"All in favor?" Miklosz said. Five hands were raised. "Carried. Delmore?"

"I am pleased to report"—Delmore Rankin brushed back his blond cowlick—"that I have all the publishers' checks in the bank, including one from my own notoriously stingy company."

"Public relations?" Miklosz questioned, turning to Vergil Yount.

"Every reporter I know will be there," Vergil said, "and I know them all. And politicians too, a necessary evil. A bank of phones and some typewriters set up, and a big batch of releases. This is the biggest event in the history of crosswords and it will get all the publicity it deserves."

"Brundage?"

"I have a well-trained corps of clean-cut boys and girls, all properly dressed, red blazers and ties, short hair, everything. Traffic and directions will be handled with maximum efficiency. I do run a big business, you know."

"Good," said Miklosz. "Lila?"

"Hospitality is set. Good-quality snacks and wine will be available at slightly inflated prices. Excellent coffee with real cream, choice of teas, soft drinks. Everything is under control." Nobody doubted that.

"The contest committee, Caroline?"

"The rules were mailed to each contestant last Wednesday," Caroline Trimble whispered. "The solvers puzzle will be about as hard as the *New York Times* Sunday puzzle, but a little smaller, conventional type, no more than six puns and/or anagrams. One mistake disqualifies the contestant, and neatness *counts*. The first three to finish *perfectly*, win."

"With all these contestants, won't some be farther away from the timekeeper than others?" Kantor asked.

"We'll have little tables with time stampers scattered throughout the area. For handicapped people, we'll have runners. Everyone will be treated with *absolute* fairness."

"How will you know if a professional tries to enter?" Brundage asked. "Even to a top pro, twenty-five thousand is a lot of money."

"Between us, we know all the pros," Miklosz said. "Besides, they're all a pretty honorable lot. It's inherent in the field."

"There's one pro you *don't* know," Brundage said. "Hannibal."

"He won't enter," Giles Sullivan said.

"How can you know that?" Brundage pressed.

"I have represented him on occasion," Giles said.

"Oh, my God," Caroline Trimble said softly. "He's the one you retained to make up the contest puzzles, isn't he?"

"I'm sorry, Caroline," Giles said. "I can't reveal the name of the constructor to anyone. That was your rule, you may remember."

"I knew it," Caroline wailed. "I just knew it." She began crying softly. "I was counting *so* on winning third prize in one of the contests. Counting...He's *so* unfair. I can't...I need the money so..."

Miklosz shifted his chair closer and held the sobbing woman. After a minute she straightened up and wiped her nose. "I know, Caroline," Miklosz said. "We all need the money except Harvey Brundage. It's all right. If it's hard for you, it's hard for everyone else too. You're one of the best; we all know that."

"He's right, Caroline dear," Giles said. "Cheer up. The constructor I retained—and I'm not saying it was Hannibal—understood that all the clues were to follow the rules exactly. The answers too."

"You mean you know who Hannibal really is?" Rankin asked. Giles nodded.

"I know who he isn't," Brundage blurted out. "He isn't any of the major professionals. I had them investigated."

"What do you mean, investigated?" Janos Miklosz asked.

"I hired the best detective agency in the city. They spent weeks checking, and I assure you, it isn't any of the working pros."

"Couldn't they trace his fees from the magazines?" Rankin asked. "He has to endorse his checks."

"He doesn't get checks; his cover letter tells which charity to make out the check to."

"He must be hiding from something," Lila said, "or from somebody."

"If he is," Kantor said, "he's very good at it. He's been constructing puzzles, publicly at least, for almost twenty years."

"There's one other thing," Brundage said. "Your rules, Caroline, say the decision of the judges is final. I want you to make sure I'm treated fairly. Some of the judges don't like me."

"I wonder why," Lila Quinn needled. "If we had to get judges who didn't *hate* you, Harvey, we'd end up with, maybe, your mother and your father, if we knew who he was, and I'm not too sure your mother would qualify."

Brundage stood abruptly. "I've heard about enough out of you, *Mrs. Isadore Cohen.* You'll live to regret—"

"Irwin had his name changed legally," she said, "because of prejudice from creeps like you. But don't worry, darling; I guarantee I won't convert to Episcopal at *your* church, so relax."

"I have the T-shirts and other souvenirs ready for delivery on Wednesday," Miklosz said, "so everything seems to be all set. Let's adjourn. We'll meet here at six sharp a week from today for a final check and to take care of any problems that come up in the last few days before the big event."

"Before we adjourn," Giles said, "I'd like to suggest that we meet at my home rather than here at the club. I know you all work during the day and it will be late before you get home to supper, so we'll dine immediately after our meeting. Ping is an excellent cook; I can promise you a good meal. And I would enjoy your company; I tire of dining alone."

There were grateful murmurs all around. Norbert Kantor casually inquired, "Have you decided on the menu yet, Giles?"

"We'll begin with marinated artichoke hearts, spinach soup, and endive salad. The entree will be trout amandine, with creamy mashed potatoes and braised salsify. Dessert will be meringues filled with whipped cream and covered with shaved chocolate, finishing with espresso and sambuca."

Kantor smiled his thanks. "It was typically considerate of you, Giles, to plan a meal I could eat."

"The pleasure of my guests is my pleasure," Giles said.

"There's one more thing I'd like to discuss," Brundage said. "The contest rules say that any reference books and any printed matter may be consulted during the contest. If you can use books, why not written notes, typed sheets, other forms of recording? I think this rule was included to help the publishers sell books."

"It won't help," Giles said, "to prepare blocks of crossed words. Each puzzle will have a theme, and no one can possibly know in advance what the theme is."

"Why just printed notes?" Harvey pressed. "In this modern day and age..."

"Let's talk straight," Vergil Yount said bluntly. "It's because we don't want you bringing in a portable computer with a ten-megabyte memory so in one second you can display every nine-letter word in the English language with second letter e and fifth letter h."

"Where did you hear—?" Brundage's face reddened.

"Publishing is a small world," Delmore Rankin said. "If you hire a programmer and six full-time researchers, word gets around."

"That's why we told Caroline to make sure it said printed matter, creep," Lila Quinn said. "She's so straight, it would never occur to her that even you would try to win by cheating with a computer."

"It's not cheating," Harvey insisted. "If you allow reference material, it should include all types."

"That's fallacious, Harvey," Kantor said. "The time spent looking up a word will almost guarantee not finishing in the money. But a powerful computer, properly programmed, can produce a list of possible words in a second. No talent or skill is required."

"That describes you, Harvey," Lila said. "You've gone as far as you can go with your money, but you'll never be the best even if you live to be one hundred. If two more fast kids come up, you won't even be in the top twenty in the club."

"That's where you're wrong, Lila," he said viciously. "You think I have only one string to my bow? Well, you're dead wrong. I'm going to win both the solvers contest and the constructors contest. And none of you will come anywhere near the top ten."

"What are you going to do, Harvey?" Miklosz smiled. "Put out a contract on all of us?"

"You'll see," Harvey muttered. "Starting tomorrow."

"**H**AVE ANY OF MY GUESTS ARRIVED YET?**" GILES SUL-
livan inquired as he handed his black homburg to his
butler.

"Mr. Miklosz and Mrs. Quinn are in the drawing room,
sir," Oliver said. "I opened a bottle of the second-best
amontillado."

"Oliver, you are an unmitigated snob."

"Thank you, sir. One does one's best." He took Sullivan's cashmere chesterfield and white silk scarf. "I do
wish you wouldn't carry *that* cane in the street, sir."

"It saved my life once, Oliver."

"If it should come apart in public, sir . . . It is, legally,
a concealed weapon."

"Unarmed combat is for younger men, Oliver," Giles
said with a sigh. "The reflexes go first."

"I *had* noticed that, sir, last week when Ping dropped
the tray. One of the glasses almost hit the floor before
you caught it."

"Is Ping prepared, Oliver? I want the slivered almonds
very crisp this time."

"All goes apace, sir. The wines are being properly

14

chilled. Ping requests that the dinner be completed before nine."

"Are soap operas now intruding on the evening hours?"

"A two-hour special, sir, four-handkerchief rating. Ping would be quite put out if he missed the opening advertisements."

"We will *not* gulp our food, Oliver, but you may reassure Ping—the meeting should be short. Did you arrange for the limousine to pick up Miss Macintosh?"

"The lady called this morning, sir, just after you left. She will be driving down, not flying."

"In her surplus jeep?" Giles exploded. "All the way from Vermont? I distinctly told her she must never do that again."

"Miss Macintosh is quite stubborn, sir. A failing of the Scottish race, I understand."

"I'm going upstairs to dress," Giles said. "When Miss Macintosh arrives, tell her I want to see her at once. She will learn that the Irish can be just as stubborn as the Scots."

"If you say so, sir," said Oliver politely.

 **4**

"**W**HAT ARE YOU SO NERVOUS ABOUT?" LILA QUINN asked. "I thought the import-export business is doing good."

"Business is not bad," Janos Miklosz said, "and collections are not good, but I'm used to that."

"So why are you biting your new cigarette holder like you're trying to kill it?"

"It's my old one, Lila. I cleaned it thoroughly and even reamed out the inside to get rid of the tobacco taste, but there's still a little left."

"You're also not answering my questions, Janos."

"I'm no more nervous than you are, Lila. The big contests are only three days away."

"That's your third glass of wine, Janny. Contests never bothered you before."

"It's the biggest prize in the history of the club, Lila. Besides, you look pretty worried yourself."

They stared at each other. Lila broke the silence. "Did you get a funny phone call, Janny?"

"From Bulgaria, all I get is funny phone calls."

She looked at him sadly. "So you got one too, Janny? That's what I figured. Mine sounded like a robot."

He turned away for a moment, then looked straight into her eyes. "It was a voice synthesizer, Lila. So if you taped it, you couldn't prove who made the call."

"I don't need proof, Janny." She gulped her wine. "So that's how the creep thinks he's going to win."

"Not thinks, Lila," Miklosz said. "I'm seriously considering withdrawing from the contests. Or if that's too obvious, I'll make a mistake. On purpose."

"That bad, Janny?"

"Worse. He must have been investigating me for months. Sometimes a man has to do things.... But you, Lila? What could you have done that...?"

"We all have our little basket of goodies, Janny. Nobody's an angel."

"Caroline Trimble? That mouse?"

"You can't tell by looks, Janny. You can bet your life we all got phone calls."

Delmore Rankin entered, sat down, and poured a full glass of the sherry. "You didn't ask how I am, Delmore," Lila said, "but I'll tell you anyway. In one five-letter word, lousy. I also got a phone call."

"Also?"

"Don't try to hide it, Delmore; I can tell from your face. Also means *also*. You too. And Janos. And the other three, guaranteed. What are you going to do?"

"I thought a tranquilizer cocktail, in vodka. It's supposed to be easy."

"You could just throw the contest, Delmore," Miklosz said. "That's what I'll probably do."

"That's another way of dying, Janny boy," Vergil Yount said, walking heavily into the room. "How about praying that he gets hit by a car?"

"That kind never has accidents," Lila said. "But does it have to be an *accident*? I will personally be slave for a month to anyone who does the job. I'll even do windows."

"You always get right to the heart of the problem, Lila," Yount said. "Unfortunately, we're all word people. All talk and no action."

"*Giles* is still pretty tough," Miklosz said. "I heard stories about when he was in the O.S.S."

"No good, Janos," Delmore said. "He's not competing. But why are you concerned, Vergil? You're nationally syndicated; money can't be that critical for you."

"Eight children, three ex-wives, and their vicious lawyers don't leave a man much. There have been times when I was forced to imbibe caramel-colored grain neutral spirits instead of honest sour-mash bourbon. I have to put *something* aside for when my brain has become completely marinated."

Oliver showed Caroline Trimble in. He glanced at the table and, without a word, went to the sideboard and opened two more bottles of sherry. No one said anything until he closed the door behind him.

"Caroline," Vergil said, "you look like you haven't slept for a week. Here's a sherry. Drink it down; it'll do you good."

"That monster," she whispered. "That—bastard! If only my father were alive."

Yount put his big paw over her tiny hand. "I'll protect you, Caroline love, and so will the others. We're all in the same boat, though I don't understand"—he smiled gallantly—"how a perfect lady such as yourself could possibly have any secret that could cause you such pain."

"It's not just what you did that counts, Vergil, or what could happen to you if it got out," Lila said. "It's how you feel about it's being made public. It doesn't even have to be you; it could be someone you love."

"It could even be something that happened to you," Delmore said. "Something you had no control over, like rape. Or incest."

At this Caroline burst into tears. Vergil patted her hand helplessly.

Lila moved to the side of Caroline's chair and put her arm around the crying woman's shoulder. "When everything gets to be too much, Caroline," Lila said, "it's okay to cry. I've done plenty of it in my time; I know what it's like. But I also know—and I'm old enough to be your mother, so you can take my word—that things change. Tomorrow? Who knows? A brick could drop on his head, or a stroke. . . . With my best wishes, God will punish him, guaranteed."

"Ah, Professor," Yount said as Norbert Kantor entered the room. "I have an ethical question for you."

Kantor took in the tableau with his sad brown eyes. His face was gray. "The Commandment?" he asked. "Thou shalt not kill?"

"You're far ahead of us, Norbert," Yount said, "as usual. But—an alternative? What does the Talmud say about throwing a contest?"

"Nothing specific, Vergil, but dishonesty in any form is not kosher. However, the Commandment does not mean you cannot take life; it means you must not commit murder."

"There's always a hitch," Lila said. "It's hard to be a Jew."

5

ISABEL MACINTOSH KNOCKED ONCE, LIGHTLY, AND walked into Sullivan's bedroom. She pulled his hands from his tie down to her waist, then held him tightly, cheek to cheek, like dear friends, like old lovers. "Oliver said you wanted to see me as soon as I got in. That's sweet. I missed you too."

Giles was torn between wanting to lecture her and needing to hold her even more closely. Lecturing could wait, he decided. "It is just plain stupidity," he said, "at our age, to live so far apart."

"I agree, darling," Isabel said. "You can live in my cottage as long as you're nice. Which, I hope, is as long as we both shall live."

"You left out the first part, Isabel—holy matrimony."

"I won't be a formal chattel, dear, but I'll wash if you'll dry."

"I can't live in Vermont, Isabel; you know that. I have too many commitments in New York. Marry me, darling; this house is big enough for ten."

"My cottage is just the right size for two, and it's in the woods. And *I* have a schoolful of girls who need *me*."

"Why are you so stubborn, Macintosh? There are lots of others who can take your place."

"You're so right, Sullivan. I'll send you one of them to marry."

"I'm not talking about personal feelings, Macintosh; no one is indispensable in his work."

"I agree wholeheartedly, Sullivan. Tell Winston to get someone else to consult with so you can live with me and be my love."

He glared at her. "I have bested some of the greatest prosecutors in America. Why can't I ever win with you?"

"You do, darling, all the time. And so do I. The best way. We both win, together." She walked to the door and snapped the lock. "It's been eight weeks, Giles...."

"We'll be late for dinner, Isabel," he said weakly.

"We have a head start, darling. Your tie isn't tied."

 **6**

H**ARVEY** B**RUNDAGE** ENTERED THE ROOM, WEARING HIS hearty smile. He picked up a bottle from the table and checked the label. "The best," he said. "Giles has good taste. Is there an unopened bottle around?"

"Worried, darling?" Lila asked. "Why?"

"Nothing really specific, Lila," Brundage said. "But sometimes people get so jealous they do—foolish things."

"I can't imagine anyone being jealous of you, Harvey," Vergil said. "Whatever for?"

"Well, I *am* going to win both contests." He chuckled falsely. No one joined him. "Is there any doubt of that?" he asked, too loudly. He looked around, his eyes stopping at each face. No one moved. No eyes met his.

"We have a saying in Yiddish," Lila said. "It's 'You should live so long.' It sounds like a wish for a long life. It isn't."

"I hope no one would be so foolish as to think . . ." He was still smiling. "I am a very careful man. Enough said. But why are you all so hostile? Shouldn't you be happy that a fellow director . . . ?"

"Why did you do it, Harvey?" Kantor asked, his face lined with worry. "The money means nothing to you."

"Do it? Do what, Kantor?"

"Don't waste your breath, Norbert," Miklosz said, his teeth tightly clenched on his cigarette holder. "Let him win. We lived without the money before; we'll live without it for another year. Our time will come."

"Very wise," Harvey said with a twisted smile. "But don't count on next year either, Janos. It might be very nice if I won two years in a row. And next year we'll allow computers—right, guys?"

"You bastard," Caroline Trimble said. She did not whisper.

 7

THE OTHERS STAYED BACK SO THAT BRUNDAGE WAS
the first to enter the dining room. They waited until he
was seated, then Lila and Caroline took chairs on the
opposite side of the round table. Norbert sat next to Lila
and Delmore next to Caroline. Vergil took the seat near
Norbert, and Janos the one next to Delmore, leaving
Brundage with one empty seat on either side. He colored
slightly, then looked aside.

Oliver approached Miklosz and whispered, "I had
planned that Miss Macintosh should sit next to Mr. Sullivan, sir."

"No," said Miklosz firmly, emphasizing the word with
a jab of his ivory holder.

Oliver looked the question at Vergil Yount. "No," said
Yount, equally firmly, settling his bulk immovably in the
chair.

Giles and Isabel entered the dining room. Giles took
in the situation at a glance, then quietly steered Isabel to
the chair on Brundage's left, next to Miklosz, and sat
down himself, on Brundage's right, near Vergil Yount.
Oliver served the marinated artichokes at once and opened
two bottles of pale yellow Reisling.

24

"I am so pleased to be dining here tonight," Isabel said. "Giles has told me all about you. I'm Isabel Macintosh, an old friend of the Sullivan family." Giles went clockwise around the table, introducing them all to Isabel. "This is Janos Miklosz our Hungarian charmer." Miklosz kissed her hand. "*Enchanté*, madame."

"Delmore Rankin, our brightest young star."

"How do you do," Delmore said.

"Caroline Trimble, our super-organizer."

"I am truly pleased to meet you," Caroline said.

"Lila Quinn, the world's greatest blitz-Scrabble player." Lila studied Isabel for a moment, then said, "Do it, lady. Don't hesitate." Isabel, surprised, nodded slightly.

"Norbert Kantor, our resident genius."

"I hope you're enjoying this weekend, Miss Macintosh," Norbert said.

"Vergil Yount, whose column you have no doubt read."

"And disagreed with, I hope, Miss Macintosh; you seem to be too nice to be on my side." Yount grinned.

"And last, on your right, Harvey Brundage, head of one of our largest arbitraging firms."

"This is indeed an honor," Harvey said, beaming.

"I hope to get to know you all better by the end of the evening." Isabel smiled around the table.

"It will be our pleasure, Miss Macintosh," Vergil said. "I know that Giles will be busy just before each contest. May I have the honor or escorting you to the club?"

"Won't you have last-minute practicing to do, Mr. Yount?" Isabel said.

"I don't think so," he said heavily, with a glance at Brundage.

Oliver cleared the dishes and served the soup. "Janny," Lila said sharply, "are you going to chew that empty cigarette holder after every course?"

"I'm a little nervous today," he said. "You understand." He placed the ivory cylinder alongside his forks as he picked up his spoon. "Delicious soup, Giles. How does a Chinese cook know French cuisine so well?"

"He worked at the Savoy for several years," Giles said.

"Is that where you stole him from?" Yount asked.

"Actually, Oliver found him," Giles said.

"Who found Oliver?" Lila asked.

"He was batman for the British officer with whom I worked. After that brave man—disappeared, I inherited Oliver. Fortunately for me." Oliver nodded in agreement.

"I'd give anything for a butler," Lila said, "and a cook like Ping. This is the best soup I've ever tasted."

Oliver placed the soupbowls on a tray. He came back promptly with a trolley and put the heated plates in front of each diner, serving the mashed potatoes and the long white salsify roots. As Oliver finished, Ping, the thin old Chinese cook, pushed in another cart, which held a silver platter of perfectly broiled trout, crisp and brown, covered with slivers of roasted almonds. Oliver deftly placed one trout and a sprig of parsley on each person's plate, opened two bottles of golden Meursault, and withdrew with both serving carts.

There were little expressions of appreciation as each of Gile's guests cut into the crunchy skin of the trout, and for a moment there was silence, the highest compliment to a cook. Then Isabel, remembering her duties as a hostess, turned to Harvey Brundage, on her right.

"I just love to salsify," she said, "don't you? Actually, Giles introduced me to it; it's not easy to find in New England."

Brundage began to respond, then abruptly clawed at

his collar. His mouth was wide open, yawning, gasping for breath, half-chewed food dribbling down his chin. His face became red, his throat swelled, and his head fell forward, slamming into his plate.

8

"**W**HY ARE GILES AND MISS MACINTOSH IN THERE SO long?" Caroline Trimble asked.

"Lieutenant Faber has a thousand-watt light shining in their eyes," Delmore Rankin said, "and is beating them with a rubber hose."

"I'm serious," Caroline said. "He made *us* go in one by one. Why did he take the two of them together?"

"The old school tie," Vergil Yount said. "Giles's father was a cop, Giles's brother, Percival, used to be chief of detectives, and Giles himself has lots of friends on the force from when he was a practicing criminal lawyer."

"Did you say Percival?" Delmore asked. "With a name like that, how did he ever become a cop?"

"It is probable," Norbert said, "that he became a cop because of his father. When Giles chose law, it fell on Percival to carry on the family tradition. I'm certain that it was *because* of his name that Percival got his reputation."

Delmore looked puzzled.

"You weren't born in New York," Norbert asked, "were you?"

"No," Delmore said. "I came here about ten years ago, after high school."

"That explains it," Norbert said. "With a name like that, in Hell's Kitchen, where the Sullivans grew up, you had to become ... When Percival was a patrolman he made very few arrests, yet his district had very little crime. If Percival did arrest a lawbreaker, he never went to trial; he confessed."

"I don't understand," Delmore said.

"Percival had a simple motto: You commit a crime; you get punished. If the law didn't do it, Percival did."

"In this day and age?" Delmore was shocked.

"It wasn't this day and age then," Norbert explained gently. "And it worked. Percival isn't as tall as Giles, but he's twice as wide, and his fists are as big as your head."

"Sounds like a real monster to me."

"Don't get the idea he was just a gorilla, Delmore; he was very smart. He studied hard and took all the promotion tests; there was a lot of brass who felt the way he did, and they pushed him. When he was chief, New York was a much safer place than it is now. He backed his men all the way, including one guy he shouldn't have. The politicians forced him into early retirement, but while he was in charge, he never bent."

"Evidently he still has a lot of influence."

"The men who worked under him would have walked through fire for him," Norbert said. "It's only natural they treat Percival Sullivan's big brother with kid gloves."

"That's discrimination," Caroline was indignant. "Why should I be a suspect? I was sitting as far from Harvey Brundage as possible. Whatever could Giles be telling the lieutenant?"

"About us, you mean?" Lila Quinn asked.

"About all of us," Caroline said. "You don't think Giles

knows about the phone calls, do you?"

"Not unless he bugged the drawing room," Vergil said. "But that's not his style."

"I don't think *anyone* should know about the phone calls," Delmore said. "Especially Giles. He's very good at worming things out of people."

"Giles can't tell on us," Caroline said. "He's our attorney."

"Not quite," Janos said. "He's the attorney for the club, not for us personally."

"The less he knows, the better," Lila said firmly. "All agreed?" The others nodded.

"What did *you* tell the police, Lila?" Caroline twisted her handkerchief into a tight rope.

"The same as you, Carrie," Lila Quinn said. "I told him I didn't see anything, I didn't hear anything, I don't know anything, and that if I did, I wouldn't tell them anything."

"You *didn't*!" Caroline looked shocked.

"Why not?" Lila looked around at the other directors. "Whoever did it—and I know it was one of you, because I know I didn't—God bless you and keep you from harm."

"It is wrong to commit murder, Lila," Norbert Kantor said. "Please don't make a joke of it."

"I wouldn't call it murder, Professor," Vergil Yount said, "any more than I'd call the extermination of a rabid dog a murder."

"I feel very good that Harvey Brundage is dead," Janos Miklosz said. "Vergil put it properly, only not strong enough. Brundage was much worse than a poor sick dog; he knew what he was doing to us, and he enjoyed it."

"What makes you think it was one of us, Lila?" Delmore said, sipping his sherry.

"Who else?" Lila asked. "Ping? Maybe if he went suddenly crazy, but I see him using a cleaver, not poison, particularly in something he cooked himself."

"Why did you say poison, Lila?" Yount asked. "We don't have the autopsy yet. It could turn out to be a stroke or a heart attack."

"Never," Lila said. "I used to help Irwin in the store after the kids were big, and a couple of times a year somebody comes in with a terrible indigestion—could he have a glass of water and a Bromo-Seltzer?—which turns out to be a heart attack. So I've seen plenty of those. You think if the medical examiner told the cops it was a heart attack, we would have been interrogated for so long? This was cyanide, guaranteed."

"How could you know that?" Caroline asked, shrinking away from Lila Quinn.

"Did you see his face?" Lila said. "Practically deep purple. And how fast he died? A few bites of the trout, and bingo."

"Could it not have been a slow-acting poison," Vergil asked, "administered hours or even days before he died? And then he just happened to pass away during our dinner?"

"Very doubtful," Norbert Kantor said. "Not only is it too big a coincidence for a working hypothesis, but with slow-acting poisons, such as arsenic, there is a slow decline in health rather than a rapid—" He stopped suddenly, then said apologetically, "I have some friends in the Chemistry Department. I also read detective stories."

"Couldn't the poison have been in the soup? Or in the artichokes?" Miklosz asked.

"If it was cyanide," Kantor said, "no. Assuming it was a solid, sodium or potassium cyanide, it would have been visible on Harvey's plate. If it was dissolved in the artichoke marinade or in the soup, we would all be dead by now. If it was in liquid or gaseous form, hydrocyanic acid, the odor would have given it away. The almond smell, you know. So it must have been in the trout."

"And it had to be solid," said Miklosz, "probably in a capsule, so it wouldn't dissolve right away and smell too strong. Brundage would never notice it mixed in with the pieces of toasted almond. Lila is always right."

"I'm not always right," she said, "but I'm never wrong. Completely, I mean."

"I can see that a quiet person, like Ping," Caroline said, "wouldn't be the sort of person who could kill anyone, so..."

Delmore grinned. "Or a shy person like Miss Caroline Trimble?"

"Well, I didn't mean it exactly that way"—Caroline blushed—"but, yes, certain kinds of people just could not bring themselves to commit—any kind of violence."

"I'm not accusing you, Caroline," Vergil said seriously, "but anyone in the newspaper business knows that any kind of person can commit murder if the motive is strong enough. Poison is a woman's weapon."

"Or a word pusher's weapon," Lila said. "Which is what we all are." She stared at her colleagues over her glasses, but no one's eyes met hers.

"What I was trying to say before"—Caroline broke the silence—"was that I didn't think Ping *could* have done it. He just brought in the platter on a hot table, that's all. He couldn't know who would get which trout."

There was a moment of silence, then Yount exploded with laughter. "The butler did it? THE BUTLER DID IT? Oh, my goodness gracious, Caroline, you have made this a frabjous day. First, Harvey the Rotter gets his comeuppance, then I become an active participant in a genuine classic."

"Caroline's logic is unassailable," Kantor said. "No one else had any control over who got which fish."

"Oliver must be seventy," Delmore said. "Isn't that a little old for a killer?"

"Giles is sixty-eight," Miklosz said, "and I can easily see him killing someone with his bare hands."

"That's different," Yount said. "Giles was a trained athlete. He almost won a medal for fencing in the thirty-six Olympics. He did some very dangerous stuff in the war; I looked him up. Oliver is just a butler, a fat little old butler."

"You heard what Giles told us at supper," Delmore said. "He got Oliver after a brave British officer was killed. How does an American inherit a British soldier? And why? It could only be that Giles was doing the same dangerous work, and that Oliver was part of it. I'll bet that if you checked, you'd find that Oliver is an expert with guns, knives, ropes—that sort of thing. You can't tell by looks."

"Poison too?" Caroline asked.

"Especially poison," Delmore said. "They all carried a capsule of—guess what—potassium cyanide in case they were captured. I'll bet they didn't all turn them in after the war was over, either."

"But why?" Miklosz asked. "I'm sure Oliver never saw Brundage before."

"Maybe Giles got a telephone call too, last week," Lila said. "Oliver must have overheard it. Servants always listen in. He wanted to protect his master. Oliver is very loyal. I can tell."

"But Giles isn't competing in the contests," Kantor said. "Why should Brundage blackmail him?"

"I can think of two reasons," Caroline said. "Three. The way Giles threatened Brundage last week when he

33

was yelling at Lila. Brundage didn't like that at all, I could tell. Then maybe he was afraid that Giles would try to protect us from Harvey's blackmail."

"You mean Brundage was afraid *Giles* would kill him?" Miklosz asked incredulously.

"That's possible," Caroline said, "but what I had in mind is that Giles is a lawyer, and very influential. Maybe Harvey was afraid Giles could figure out a way to stop him. Legally, I mean. Like having him arrested."

"Let's not forget," Yount said quietly, "that Giles was a criminal lawyer, so he must have many contacts with the underworld. Giles could easily *arrange* to have Harvey's knees broken."

"He could contract to have his neck broken just as easily," Delmore said, "but I don't see Giles hiring someone else to do the job for him. Don't let his old-fashioned politeness fool you."

"Then why would Oliver kill Brundage?" Kantor asked. "Knowing what Giles is like, I mean."

"To save Giles from having to do it," Caroline said. "It wouldn't be the first time a loyal servant sacrificed himself for his master."

"You said there were three reasons," Kantor reminded her.

"Giles knows who Hannibal is," Caroline said. "Harvey wanted the two puzzles in his hands before the contest."

"Giles would *never* do that," Kantor said.

"*You* were considering throwing the contest, Norbert," said Yount, "even though you need the money desperately. One week ago I would have sworn *you* would never do that. It depends upon the incentive, I guess." Yount gulped down his sherry and refilled his glass.

"Brundage was between Giles and Miss Macintosh," Miklosz said. "If Oliver is as loyal as we think, he would never put either Giles or the lady under suspicion like that."

"He tried very hard to get me or you to move over, Janny," Yount said, "so that Brundage would not be between the two."

"But we didn't move," Miklosz said. "Why did he go ahead with his plan?"

"When else would Oliver have had a chance to kill Brundage?" Lila asked. "Do you think it would be so easy to get potassium cyanide and trout amandine together with a bunch of prime suspects in the three days left before the contests? This was his only opportunity; now or never."

"Why are we all trying so hard to say Oliver did it?" Kantor asked. "The poison didn't have to be put on the fish *before* it was served."

"I guess we all realized that subconsciously," Delmore said. "It would have been easy for Giles to slip the capsule onto Harvey's plate. We just don't want to face up to the fact that temperamentally, and by training, Giles is the most likely suspect."

"My money is on Macintosh," Lila said. "With her face, even at her age she could look into Harvey's eyes and he wouldn't notice if she slipped a sixteen-ton weight into his lap."

"Why would Miss Macintosh do that?" Kantor asked.

"You couldn't tell?" Lila looked at him in amazement. "She's in love with Giles."

"Is Giles?" Kantor asked. "With her, I mean."

"Even worse," Lila said. "So you see, it's quite possible one of us didn't do it."

"Giles is one of us," Caroline said. "And for all practical purposes, so is Miss Macintosh."

"Yeah," Lila said. "So I guess one of us *did* do it. Although the butler would have been neater."

9

"Do the cops really think Oliver did it?" Delmore asked Giles. "Is that why they saved him for last?"

"You must understand how the police work," Giles said. "Oliver was the one who distributed the food. No one else could have known which serving Harvey Brundage would get. So, although they have no motive yet, they wanted to get all of our statements together to see if anything Oliver said would be contradicted by any of us."

"Does that mean we're all in the clear?" Vergil asked.

"Not really," Giles said. "They're not ready to accuse anyone or to clear anyone yet. After Oliver, Isabel and I are second on the list, then you and Janny, Delmore and Norbert, and last, Caroline and Lila."

"In order of distance from Brundage?" Norbert said. "That means the poison—it was poison, wasn't it?"

Giles nodded. "Cyanide, potassium cyanide."

"Then they believe the cyanide was put into the fish during the meal, *after* Ping brought the hot tray in."

"If it was put in before," Giles said, "Ping would have to be the killer; the trout was served hot from the grill.

But then how could Ping know Harvey would get the poisoned fish?"

"Do they think you or Miss Macintosh could have done it?" Norbert asked.

"At this time it's a matter of probabilities," Giles answered. "They did ask if Vergil reached across me at any time, or if Janny reached across Miss Macintosh."

"I didn't," Janos said. "At least I don't think I did. Did I?" He turned pleading eyes to Isabel.

"No," she said. "You didn't. But everyone, myself included, did reach for something toward the center of the table—salt, pepper, wine—it's normal."

"But even if I did," Caroline said, "I couldn't reach Harvey's plate. And there were bottles and everything in the middle of the table. I couldn't even *see* his plate."

"Relax, Carrie," Lila said. "If you're going to take every little thing personally, the police will be sure you're the murderer."

"'The wicked flee when no man pursueth,'" quoted Vergil.

"Nevertheless," Norbert said, "it is almost certain that one of us *did* kill Harvey Brundage. The newpapers and television will make a big story of this. Brundage was an important man in business and financial circles."

"And you're concerned about your image?" Delmore asked.

"Of course I am," Norbert said. "In the academic world a reputation must be spotless. But even more important to me is what my family and friends think of me. You should also be concerned, Delmore. Even in publishing, where chicanery is not unknown, it will do you no good to be saddled with a twelve-percent probability that you are a murderer."

"None of us would want that," Miklosz said. "You

sound as though you have something in mind."

"We have to find the murderer," Norbert said. "It's as simple as that."

"We don't have to find anything," Lila said sharply. "Harvey was a creep and a—even worse. I'm glad he's dead. We all are. Let the police do their job. If they succeed, okay. If they don't, even better."

"It's our duty," Kantor said.

"To right *every* wrong?" Delmore asked. "Or can we be selective? Maybe pick the most pressing? Or the most important? Such as preventing war?"

"There may be—if we investigate—matters uncovered," Vergil said, "which could, conceivably, cause even more, ah, difficulties than living with the slight suspicion that one *might* have been involved in the removal of a highly obnoxious bastard."

"On the other hand," Miklosz said, "if we do the investigating ourselves, we may be able to winnow out only the useful facts and leave the, uh, peripheral information in the background. If the entire investigation is left to the police, they may attach unwarranted importance to matters that have very little bearing on who killed Harvey Brundage."

Giles, slightly puzzled, was watching the interplay. "All of the directors are here," he said. "Why not take a vote?"

"Good idea," said Miklosz. "Although this is not a formal meeting, I'd like to consider it binding on all of us, so we don't work at cross purposes. Agreed, Norbert?"

"I'll abide by the consensus."

"Good. All in favor of the board of directors investigating the death of Harvey Brundage, say aye." Silence. "All opposed?" There were five loud nays. "Good. There will be no investigation by us."

Giles spoke up. "The original purpose of our getting together this evening, which everyone seems to have forgotten, was to go over the last-minute preparations for the anniversary contest weekend. It's late, and I can see we're all upset. Since the investigation has been concluded for now and we've been officially dismissed, I suggest we meet tomorrow morning, Thursday, at nine o'clock, at the club, to discuss the preparations and to allocate Harvey's responsibilities."

"Can you make that eight o'clock?" Norbert asked. "I have an eleven o'clock class."

"My boss gets mad if I get in after ten," Delmore said, "I'd like eight o'clock too."

"Can everyone get there at eight?" Miklosz asked. They all nodded. "Good. We meet in the conference room. I'll arrange coffee and Danish."

"No almond Danish for me," Lila said. "I'll take Twinkies. In a sealed package." The others gasped in shock. "I was only kidding," she protested. "I'll eat whatever is on the table. Why is everybody so uptight?"

Why indeed? Giles thought. Why indeed.

10

"IT'S UNANIMOUS, THEN," JANOS SAID. "IN THE AB-
sence of Harvey Brundage, traffic and directory service
will be handled by Miss Isabel Macintosh"—her motion
caught his eye and he amended—"by Isabel—I'll get used
to saying it soon—in payment for which she gets a free
meal on the dais with the rest of us bigshots. Given her
experience as a college dean, I know she'll do a perfect
job supervising our young guides."

"Given that she's a lot smarter than the creep ever
could be," Lila said, "and twice as clean-cut-looking, she'll
have those kids eating out of her hand in no time."

There was a soft knock at the door and Fredericks,
the club manager, walked in. "A messenger just delivered
this," he said as he handed an envelope to Giles. "In view
of the circumstances, Mr. Sullivan, I thought I should
give this to you at once; it comes from the late Mr. Brundage."

Giles tore open the envelope and removed the single
sheet. He skimmed the note quickly, then read it aloud
slowly.

"Dear Giles:

"Please read this to the entire board of directors.

"I've addressed this to you because I know you play by the rules. You are the only one I can really trust. If you are reading this, I have been murdered by one of my hypocritical fellow directors. I gave them all an opportunity to make up for their past mistakes. They did not accept my offer.

"I warned them that I was very careful. One person was too stupid and arrogant to believe me. They will all pay for their sins. I will expose each one for what he is. As an officer of the court, and a good Christian gentleman, you must turn the murderer over to the police. I am depending on you to do justice; do not fail me.

"Lest you be tempted to keep this within the clique, I have made sure that all of the club members will receive puzzles. The information in the puzzles will mean nothing now, but the meaning will be evident when the key is made public next week.

"In the event you should try to shield these criminals, one week from today a copy of this letter will be sent to the police and the media unless the killer is found and his name is announced in the headlines.

"A copy of this puzzle will accompany the letter to the newspapers, with instructions to print it. The puzzle will provide clues to the crimes committed by my dear fellow directors.

"Each day there will be a new puzzle. The day after the last puzzle appears, the solutions will be made known, along with explanations and the evidence I have collected this past year about everyone involved.

"Wherever I am, be assured that I will enjoy the tortures that my fellow directors, and particularly my killer, are enduring as they feel the nooses slowly tighten around their throats.

"There is no way to stop me. Can you imagine the publicity as, each day, fifty million crossword puzzle addicts solve the puzzles that conceal clues exposing the killer?

"If you work fast enough, you may be able to keep the rest of the world from finding out what kind of people are the directors of the Cruciverbal Club. Meanwhile, let them all suffer. They deserve every moment of it.

"Look at the bulletin board, Giles; the first puzzle is there.

"Sincerely,
"Harvey Brundage

"What's on the bulletin board, Fredericks?" Giles asked.

"A stack of puzzles, sir, all alike. It's on the challenge section. It came just before this letter, delivered by a different messenger."

"Take it off right now," Lila snapped. "Quick."

"It's too late, Mrs. Quinn. Several members have already taken copies. Besides, no one but the member whose puzzle it is can remove it; it's a bylaw."

"Please bring us seven copies of the puzzle at once," Giles commanded. "And tomorrow I will—we all will, I am sure—be here at eight o'clock, at which time please bring us seven copies of that day's puzzle."

"May I have a puzzle too?" Isabel asked.

"When did you become a crossword addict?" Giles asked.

"Exactly seven weeks ago," she replied with a straight face. "I had nothing to do one day and no one to do it with, so I turned to the puzzle page. I tried it and I liked it. I'm good too."

"A worthy challenge to your talents?" Giles said.

"Not really. As sublimation, it was less than sublime. Crosswords will never replace two-handed scrabbling."

"Why didn't you mention this sooner?"

"I was saving the surprise for Saturday. I joined the club and sent in my fee for the solvers contest."

Giles was shocked. "You can't enter the contest, Isabel."

"And why not, pray?"

"Hannibal constructed the puzzle," Caroline said. "I shouldn't have entered either."

"What's the difference who constructed it?" Isabel asked.

"Hannibal is the most fiendish constructor in the business," Delmore said. "He's clever and original, and very mysterious. I'll tell you all about him right after the meeting, what little I know."

"He breaks the rules," Caroline said. "It's almost impossible for a beginner to solve one of his puzzles. He's a sneak too. He won't let anyone know who he is."

"I don't expect to win," Isabel said, "but I thought it would be fun to try."

"It will be torture," Caroline said. "Maybe you can get your money back."

"I don't quit; Giles will tell you that."

Giles turned to Fredericks. "Please bring our newest member a copy of the puzzle too." Fredericks left.

Giles sat up straight in his chair. Somehow, where he was sitting became the head of the table. "It is clear that there is damaging information about one of the directors in each puzzle. It is probable that as an inducement to find Brundage's murderer the puzzle will not reveal clearly to the uninitiated that the accusations refer to a real person, much less specifically to one of the directors of the club. Therefore, if we do not panic, we can contain the damage. I suggest that—"

Fredericks entered without knocking. He placed the eight puzzles in front of Sullivan and turned to leave. "One moment, Arthur," Giles said. "Please post on the bulletin board, just above the pad of puzzles, an announcement that whoever turns in an *original* of the puzzle, correctly filled out, will win a free drink. Make up some chits and give them out to anyone who turns in an original. Don't bother about the accuracy; the puzzle will not be terribly difficult. Charge it all to my account."

"I'll do that right away, sir."

"Do the same when the other puzzles are delivered. There may be as many as six, but certainly no less than three."

"Yes, sir."

"Need I point out, Arthur, you are the only one other than the people seated at this table who has heard the contents of the letter?"

"In the twenty years I have been in charge, Mr. Sullivan, it has never been necessary to remind me of my duties."

"I meant no offense, Arthur, just a clarification. Thank you for your very able assistance."

After Fredericks left, Giles addressed the directors. "I think it is clear that in spite of last night's vote we will have to find the killer. Does anyone dispute that?"

"I don't disagree," Janos said. "Better one killer caught than all six of us destroyed. But how? I'm not a detective.

You're not a detective. None of us is. So where does that leave us? And in one week? Impossible."

"We are a group of exceptionally intelligent people," Kantor said, "with a variety of talents and skills."

"We're competent too," Vergil added. "We weren't elected directors just because we're good at crosswords, you know."

"And we've got a real good incentive," Lila pointed out. "If we don't solve the case, we all hang."

"Five of us have a good incentive," Caroline whispered. "The sixth will try to mess things up." She looked at her colleagues fearfully. "Or even worse."

"I don't think so," Janos said judiciously. "The killer is in a terrible bind. If the actual killer helps solve the murder, it will ensure that he or she is arrested. If the killer interferes with the investigation, or does not help actively and productively, it will arouse suspicion. That person can't even shirk. Surely there is no way he or she can suddenly lose fifty points of I.Q. without its being noticed. And if, in spite of all our efforts, we fail to find the killer, in one week the killer's secret is out, the secret that was so dreadful that Harvey was killed to conceal it. All of our secrets will be out, along with the killer's. No, as much as I want to protect the killer, I'm sure that we, the killer included, will do our best."

"But what good is our best?" Delmore asked. "I wouldn't know where to start. I don't even edit the mysteries that are published by my company."

"Giles will show us what to do," Lila said. "He comes from a family of cops and he was a top criminal lawyer for forty years."

"Somewhat less," Giles said. "I spent five years in Signal Intelligence."

"A fancy name for spying," Lila said. "Which is the clincher. You tell us what to do, Giles; we'll do it. That's the only way we have a chance."

"Actually," Giles said, "we don't have a week. We have only three days."

"The contest?" Norbert asked. "What difference does that make? We all live in New York; we'll be here after the contest is over. In fact, with the pressure of the contest gone, we'll be able to think more clearly."

"I get it," Lila said. "If the killer—we're all broke, right? Nobody lies about that—if he wins one contest, he's got twenty-five grand to play with. If he wins both—and he could; we're the best in the club—he's got fifty. With that kind of dough, if the killer is the winner, and we don't know who he is, Monday morning he certifies both checks, one minute later his lawyer transfers the dough to Brazil or wherever, and by Monday noon he's gone."

"Precisely, Lila," Giles said.

"Can't the club stop the checks if the winner certifies them?" Caroline asked.

"No way," Vergil said. "First of all, it's likely there will be two winners. Which one is the killer? Maybe neither? Second, if I win, and the killer hasn't been arrested yet, I'm going to certify my check immediately and, maybe, head for the hills. Even though I know I'm not the killer, I don't want to be around when Brundage's, uh, information hits the headlines."

"What makes you so sure, Lila," Norbert asked, "that all of the prizes will be won by us? We're good, but three of us—Delmore, Caroline, and Vergil—have never placed before. None of us has ever won a first—yet. Based on what I see around the club, we all have a very good chance, but it's not guaranteed. Are you going to hold all checks and not give them out on Sunday night when the prizewinners are announced? Some of our members have a long trip home. Are you going to make them come back to collect their winnings or wait for the mail?"

"Not only that," Vergil said. "The television reporters and the newspaper photographers will want to get to the winners."

"There is the legal aspect too," Giles said. "The printed rules state that the prizes will be awarded at the closing ceremony. It's a binding agreement we entered into with each contestant when we accepted the entrance fee. The checks *must* be given out that night."

"So the deadline is Sunday night," Isabel said. "Just before the winner gets his check. Or checks."

"You don't have to be involved in this, Isabel," Giles said. "You came here for a holiday; no need to be embroiled in a homicide."

"You'd be surprised at what a dean of faculty becomes embroiled in," Isabel said. "I don't have to be involved; I want to be involved. All of you need a disinterested party around desperately. I think you need someone who, although she likes you all, can look upon you as suspects and potential murderers without past relationships getting in the way."

"Even if Giles is the killer?" Lila asked gently.

"Giles is *not* the killer," Isabel said flatly. "On my life."

"We were discussing the possibility last night," Lila pressed. "It *is* possible. Ask Giles."

"I won't," Isabel said, not looking at Giles. "If you can think Giles is the killer, you might as well suspect me too."

"We did," Lila said. "It's possible. If you're both in it together, we're all sunk."

ACROSS

1 Domicile
5 Provincial college
11 Method
14 In the same place: L. abbr.
15 Comfortably warm
16 Anger
17 Bits of information
19 ___-la-la
20 Style of jazz
21 Wearing apparel
23 Young dog
26 Numerical datum: abbr.
28 Which thing?
29 Possess
30 Genghis
31 Anchors
32 Greek vowel
33 Strong as ___
34 Find a cure
35 Affirmative
36 Upper part of a galosh
38 Father
41 Mountain goat
43 Midwestern state
44 Freeze
45 Competitor
47 Mischiefmakers
48 Be aware of
49 Dyeing apparatus
50 Leg joint
51 Blurry
52 Armed ship
54 Animal's foot
55 Acquire: Scot.
56 Impenetrable barrier
62 Rely: abbr.
63 A Beatle
64 Monster
65 Petrol
66 One of the Seven Dwarfs
67 Was roused

DOWN

1 Possessive pronoun
2 Japanese sash
3 Thousandth of an inch
4 Fit to be eaten
5 Cease
6 Charged particle
7 Servicewoman: abbr.
8 Refuse receptacle
9 Wading bird
10 Injection, for short
11 Denial
12 Debt
13 Leavening agents
18 Policeman
22 "One a penny, ___ penny..."
23 Milk serum
24 Detest
25 Politico's ploy
26 Drive away
27 Mid-April
30 Fort ___, Ky.
31 Million: prefix
33 Cain's brother
34 Chops (down)
37 Canterlike gait
39 Slip ___ (go wrong)
40 Moist, as grass
42 Hook feature
45 Unkempt
46 Large lizard
47 Chant
48 Bow obsequiously
50 Burmese tribe
51 Distant
53 Lubricates
54 Scrawny
57 Compass point: abbr.
58 Family member, for short
59 Past
60 Annoy
61 Born: Fr.

48

ILLEGAL

"This is counterproductive," Delmore said. "If were all going to suspect each other, we might as well give up right now."

"Do you want me to step aside?" Giles asked. "Let Miklosz or Lila lead?"

"No," Lila said. "You're the best we have. If you're the killer, it's already too late."

"Very well, then," Giles said. "I'll lead."

"Do your leading later," Lila said, uncapping her razor-point pen. "First things first. Pass out the puzzles and don't bother me for a while."

Norbert looked at his copy. "Standard fifteen by fifteen," he said. "Simple pattern, with just a few long words. Looks as though it won't be too hard."

"The longest words are eleven letters," Delmore said, "and there are only four of them. There's a seven-letter crossing dead center."

Yount's eyes swept the clues. "It doesn't look like any puns or anagrams were used here. I don't think there are any cryptos either."

"Strictly squaresville," Lila said. "Stop thinking and start writing. I've finished the first two lines Across already. Do I have to do all the work around here?"

They all bent over their puzzles and started writing furiously.

11

"THAT WASN'T TOO BAD," LILA SAID, CAPPING HER PEN. "As a puzzle, I mean."

Miklosz was still filling odd holes in his puzzle. "From your speed, Lila, you have to be doing only the Across words, from one to sixty seven, in numerical order."

"It's the fastest way for easy puzzles like this one. Harvey wasn't only a social disease; he was a creep as a constructor too. Look at that impossible clue I just noticed at fifty Down. Burmese tribe, would you believe it? Who could know that?"

"I knew it," Caroline said. "But he's got some really good clues too. I wouldn't have believed that Harvey was that talented."

"He's had Henry Hook for a tutor," Delmore said, "for a full year."

"That explains it," Vergil said. "Isn't seventeen Across a beauty?"

"I like the clue for thirty-six Across," Lila said.

"Will you characters stop discussing the puzzle technique," Isabel said, "and start talking about the content?"

"What content?" Delmore asked. "This is no different

from any puzzle I've ever done. Nothing in it accuses anyone of anything."

"Maybe you're supposed to analyze it a little," Giles said. "You couldn't expect a person of Harvey's caliber to construct a puzzle with a complete legal indictment spelled out, could you?"

"The theme, *Illegal*, has to be the key," said Isabel. "Why don't we list all the words that could refer to illegal acts and see what pops up?"

"If you stretch the definitions a little," Vergil said, "I can see a few right off. 'BOP,' 'BOOTLEG,' and 'ICE'— that's a slang word for kill."

"It could also be words that refer to alcoholic beverages," Caroline said. "I wonder why that didn't occur to you, Vergil."

"We all have our blind spots, my dear," he replied. "Each in our own way. We find it easier not to face certain facts."

"How about 'KNEE,'" Caroline said, "as meaning to kick a man in the groin? Or 'GAS,' as in 'to murder'?"

"Here it is," said Delmore triumphantly. "It's 'LEN-NON.' That has to refer to murder. Or, more likely, assassination."

"What about 'STOP'?" Lila said. "That means kill, at least in the mysteries I read. And 'COP,' as in 'cop a plea.'"

"Wait," said Janos. "I have it. Three words. 'MIL,' which is short for million, 'MEGA,' which *means* million, and 'KNOX,' where even the clue says 'FORT KNOX,' where all the gold is kept. One of us has stolen a million in gold from Fort Knox."

"That's not very likely, Janny," Isabel said. "If any of you are that rich, why bother entering the contests at all?"

"You're not a real fanatic yet, Isabel," Vergil said. "When you are, and I'm sure you will be soon, you'll understand the thrill of completing a really good one. Or better yet, the sense of accomplishment when you've constructed a really *great* one, where all the clues are perfectly accurate but hide the word so well that no one can solve the whole puzzle, even with references."

"I have it," Lila said. "It's not robbing banks; it's murder. Look at 'ABEL,' 'HATE,' and 'IRE.' Somebody here killed somebody, probably a brother, or at least a relative." She looked around. They all shook their heads. "Well," she said, "I didn't expect anybody to admit it."

"This time your intuition is wrong, Lila," Delmore said. "I see something else that is very interesting. Do you see 'RIVAL,' 'HYPO,' and 'BARB'? That's all drug-related. Someone hooked—that's BARB—somebody on heroin; the heroin is from HYPO, and he has a RIVAL. We have a drug dealer in our midst, and he has competition. That could even be the 'OGRE'; the guy's a monster."

"Or a giant," Caroline said, glancing at Yount.

"I'm not that tall, Caroline," Vergil said, "just wide. And alcohol is my downfall, not drugs."

"Oh, I see it now," Caroline said. "It's obviously 'MOORS,' 'OILS,' and 'KHAN.' The Moors were mixed Arab and Berber people, Khan is a high title in Moslem countries, and 'OILS' means petroleum products. Harvey is accusing one of you of doing something with the Arabs, something illegal, with a high-ranking Arab, having to do with oil."

"I think it's a woman, Caroline," Delmore said, "and it has to do with something much worse than oil. Put together 'WAC,' 'ION,' and 'TOASTY.' A woman soldier—doesn't have to be a real soldier, just someone who can legally kill people—has something to do with radiation, radioactivity, a nuclear weapon that will burn people, toast them, like a neutron bomb."

"No one here is a scientist, Delmore," Isabel said. "And I don't think Caroline and Lila were ever in the WACs, were you?" The two women shook their heads.

"But it fits," Delmore insisted. "Maybe it doesn't mean a woman. There's a missile called a WAC something. I remember reading about it."

"It was called the WAC corporal," Caroline said. "But really, how could it be one of us? I don't have access to any military information."

"Librarians have access to all sorts of information," Delmore said. "You could be passing it on. What about 'IRON CURTAIN'?"

Caroline blushed. "Working for Save the Whales does not mean that I'm a traitor. Saving the mammals is good for Americans too. I can give only very little time to it, because I'm so busy with—with all the things I have to do, so there."

"Drop that approach, Delmore," Norbert said. "I have a more promising lead. 'ASHCAN,' 'GUNBOAT,' and 'IRON CURTAIN.' Ashcan is naval slang for the depth bomb. Our navy must have developed a new kind of depth bomb, and one of us is a spy, giving the secret to the U.S.S.R."

"That's it, Norbert," Vergil said. Add 'ION' to that. And 'MIL,' short for military. That's five words that line up."

"If you're hinting at a nuclear depth bomb, forget it," Janos said. "Destroyers drop depth bombs on submarines that are directly under them. A nuclear depth bomb would destroy the submarine and the destroyers also."

"It could be dropped from an airplane," Vergil said. "In the time the bomb sank to the submarine's depth, the plane could be twenty miles away. You do importing and exporting, Janos. That's a perfect cover for transmitting secrets."

"I'm just as loyal as you are, Vergil," Janos said, becoming anxious. "Furthermore, I appreciate what it's like to live in America. You don't know what it's like over there. Try it once, and then see if you feel like spying for them."

"Gentlemen, gentlemen," Giles said. "This is not the way. We're all here to help one another help ourselves. It's not proper to accuse anyone blindly, without sufficient evidence. The clues must be here in the puzzle. We just haven't seen them yet."

"If Harvey wanted to have the general public solve the puzzles and determine what evil things he thinks we've done," Lila said, "why didn't he make it easier? If *we* haven't found the key yet, how will a layman?"

"I'm sure Harvey constructed the puzzles only to arouse interest in his accusations," Delmore said. "He would have given very broad hints in the papers he would provide with the puzzles."

"He must have thought it very clever to use puzzles to hurt us," Caroline said.

"Whether they were understood as puzzles or not," Norbert said, "he promised firm evidence from his investigations, so the dirt, whatever it is, will come out anyway."

"I can't believe that Harvey Brundage could be terribly subtle," Isabel said. "I met him only once, but he came across as a second-rate mind. Perhaps our trouble is that we're looking at the puzzle too directly, concentrating on it too hard. In the forest, where there is no earthglow, no city lights, you can see some sixth-magnitude stars. You cannot see them if you look at them directly. However, if you look a little to one side, you can see them out of the corner of your eye. Let's take a quick sideways look and see what happens."

Ten seconds later Lila looked up and said, "You can all stop looking now, because I've got it. She turned to Janos and said with pity in her voice, "You do a lot of import-export with Hungary, Poland, and Bulgaria, don't you, Janny? And maybe some of the other Warsaw Pact countries too?"

"All of them," he said guardedly.

"You pay no duty, Janny, no tax on anything you bring in? Or send out? That's what 'BOOTLEG' means, doesn't it?"

Miklosz was silent, staring down at the table.

"You also send them computers, Janny?" Lila asked softly. "Isn't that what 'SILICON CHIP' means?"

"No computers," he said. "Mining machinery and equipment."

"Harvey really stuck it to you, Janny," she said. "It jumps out of the puzzle when you look at it now. 'SILICON CHIP,' 'BOOTLEG,' and 'IRON CURTAIN.' You're smuggling computer parts into Eastern Europe, aren't you?"

Janos looked up wearily. "I guess I didn't want to see it, Lila. We all blind ourselves one way or another. But I see you're still doing what you did before, Lila; only the Across words."

"There's more about you, Janny?" she asked.

"Read the Down words, Lila," Giles said softly.

She saw Giles was serious. Her eyes swept down the puzzle. A moment later she leaned back wearily in her chair, her eyes blurred with tears.

"You mean the Across clues are for Janos," Caroline asked, "and the Down clues are for Lila?"

"That's what it looks like," Isabel said, "but which ones refer to Lila?"

"If you knew her as well as I do," Janos said, "you'd know that it couldn't be anything to do with Arabs, or murdering her brother or robbing Fort Knox. It could be only 'TAXTIME,' 'EVASIVENESS,' and 'WITH-HOLDING.' Lila is a tax evader."

"But I thought Lila was . . . I didn't know she was rich."

"She isn't," Vergil said. "The I.R.S. takes from the rich and the poor with magnificent impartiality."

"But why does it have to be Lila?" Isabel asked.

"She's the only one of us who doesn't get paid by check," Vergil said. "This sweet-looking little old lady is our local version of the old-fashioned riverboat gambler. No cheating, of course; she doesn't have to."

Crying silently, Lila said, "That bastard, that lousy creep bastard."

"I'm afraid so, darling," Vergil said. "The specter of the Internal Revenue Service strikes fear into the bravest hearts. To paraphrase an old Chinese saying, stay as far away as possible from in front of an angry woman, behind a nervous mule, and in all directions from the I.R.S."

"Today's puzzle," Giles said thoughtfully, "was aimed at two directors. If Brundage followed the same pattern, and his type is usually a rigid personality, there will be two more puzzles, each pointed at two more directors. So we can expect another puzzle early tomorrow morning and a third one on Saturday. That way, each director will have his derelictions posted on the bulletin board. I wonder why he did it this way. Wouldn't it have been easier to send all the puzzles out at once?"

"He wanted to extend the agony," Norbert said. "He wanted us to experience fearful anticipation. He expected us all to wonder and worry about who in the club figured out what and to give us a taste of what will happen a week from now. He hoped to torture us. He's succeeding, Giles, succeeding very well. Look at Janny's face. Look at Lila."

"Why did you do it, Lila," Caroline asked. "Didn't you know that sooner or later . . . ?"

"I didn't think at first. What's the difference? It's too late now."

"Maybe it isn't," Giles said. "Tell me about it, Lila. I'm still an attorney; maybe I could help."

Lila glanced around. "Not in front of everybody."

"Excuse me," Isabel said, "but it *must* be in front of us all. I know I'm not a long-term member of this group, but I *am* involved. I was sitting right next to Harvey Brundage when he was poisoned, so I'm a prime suspect, too, and I have a right to be heard. I want to help, not only to clear my name but yours as well."

"That's nice of you, Isabel," Lila said. "I appreciate the offer. But why can't I talk just to Giles? Why does it have to be in public?"

"Think, Lila," Isabel said. "What does today's puzzle say? A few words that have great meaning only to you and to Janos. We're aware of them, too, because we were expecting something like that, but to an outsider they mean nothing. At worst, the other club members will think the choice of theme was a mistake. No, it's not the puzzle that's so terrifying; it's the information that's going to be turned over to the papers and the authorities a week from today."

"That all may be true, Isabel," Janos said, "but isn't that all the more reason why I should keep my mouth shut? I'm not really proud of what I've done, aside from the danger I face."

"Isabel is right," Norbert said. "Within this group we all hold one another hostage. If information about any one

58

of us leaks out, we'll all hang, so we can be certain that whatever is said here will stay here. As for why we must have the information, it is obvious: To prevent us *all* from hanging a week from now, the killer *must* be found before the deadline."

"And you think," Janos asked, "knowing about my— my illegal deeds will help find the killer?"

"Norbert's right," Delmore said. "If one of us killed Harvey—and I'm sure one of us did—then the *motive* has to be in what we did that Harvey discovered. It is also possible that the *means* will surface at the same time. As for *opportunity*, we all had that. So tell us all about it, Janny. Don't leave out a single thing, because if you do and we don't find the killer in time, next week when Harvey's papers are made public and we find you neglected to mention one of your crimes, we'll *know* you're the killer."

"You talk first, Delmore," Janos snapped.

"I'll talk when my puzzle is posted," Delmore replied.

"You're hoping that God will destroy the vault where the puzzles are kept?" Vergil asked.

"Lightning or earthquake," Delmore said, "I don't care which. But when my time comes, I'll plead guilty with an explanation."

"As will we all," Norbert said. "I have the same impossible wish. But miracles have happened before. . . . So go ahead, Janny. Start."

"After Lila," he said.

"Across comes before Down," Lila pointed out. "Your turn."

12

"W HEN I LEFT HUNGARY," JANOS SAID, "I HAD NO idea I would never be able to go back. But when the Russians invaded, my name was on a list. I was told that because of my family it would be best if I stayed away, at least until the Russians left. But the Russians never left, not really.

"I managed to get to Brazil. With my gift for languages . . . After some odd jobs—just to eat—miner, mechanic, salesman—at a very young age I became assistant manager of a small import-export company. The owner liked me and promised that if I stayed with him and worked hard . . . But a year later his daughter married. Her husband joined the firm and was put over me.

"I arranged business matters so that I was required to go to Baltimore. There was a small group of Hungarian refugees living near Washington. They helped me to disappear."

"Then your name is not—?" Caroline asked.

"It is now and has been for many years. All of my papers are in order. They say I am an American citizen by birth. Nevertheless, a very deep investigation could prove that I am illegal. If you put a gun to my head, I would not tell you my birthname."

"Then you are afraid of being deported," Giles asked, "because you are here illegally?"

"Not really. There are more illegal aliens in this country than you could imagine. You are going to deport them all? To where? Who would take them? No, it is only *undesirable* illegal aliens who can get deported."

"That's where 'BOOTLEG,' 'IRON CURTAIN,' and 'SILICON CHIP' come in?" Isabel asked.

"Brundage must have been investigating me for a long time to find out. . . . After I had started a small business using my South American contacts, I was visited by a commercial attaché from the Czech embassy. The first thing he said to me was my sister's married name. They had traced her in spite of her having changed her name and moved to another place. He showed me a picture of her in a crowd with a recent newspaper in her hands. Her children were with her too."

"So you had no choice?" Norbert said.

"I knew what they would do."

"Are your parents still alive?" Lila asked.

"My mother. I get reports."

"So she's another hostage?" Norbert asked.

"No. After I left and the Russians came—my parents had done this under the Nazis, so they knew how—they moved to another city, not my sister's, changed names, and disappeared. The secret police will never find my mother. My sister, unfortunately, was less experienced."

"Do you know the name your mother is living under?"

"I would die before I would say it."

"Is there any way to get her out?"

"My sister, no. But my mother—I have already prepared for her to disappear into another country."

"Which is why you need the twenty-five-thousand-dollar first prize?" Isabel pressed.

"For two first prizes, I could make myself disappear, too, and the commercial attaché would never find me again."

"And your sister?" Norbert asked.

"I cannot help her. My hope is that with me gone they would have no reason to hurt her."

"What did the Czech commercial attaché want you to do?" Giles asked.

"We arranged that I would import craft goods: jams, hand-embroidered blouses, things like that. In return they wanted mining machinery. The deal was not fantastically good. I would have been suspicious if it were, but it wasn't bad, and I needed the business."

"Didn't it bother you to do business with a Communist country?" Norbert asked.

"The biggest companies in America were dealing with Russia, and still are, so who was I to . . . You must remember this was before the Russian invasion of Czechoslovakia, and at that time it was the most free of the Warsaw Pact nations and what I was bringing in and sending out was not illegal. Everything was as shown on the manifest, duties paid, all very proper."

"Then they put the squeeze on?" Vergil asked.

"Not yet. My business built up slowly over the years with Romania, Poland, and East Germany until everything I did involved the Warsaw Pact countries. I even did business with Hungary."

"So why didn't you become powerful and rich?" Delmore asked.

"They were controlling me. Every time I hired someone—Can you imagine how hard it is to get a good business head who speaks several Central European languages?

You think Rumanian is the least bit like Polish? Or German like Bulgarian? Or Hungarian like anything in the world? Every time I hired someone, business disappeared to the point I couldn't even meet payroll. So I stayed a one-man business, making a living, but not able to grow or to be financially secure."

"Nothing illegal so far," Norbert said. "So what gave Brundage such power over you? Were you bootlegging computer chips into Iron Curtain countries?"

Janos hesitated, then spread his hands in resignation. "Worse. I was forced to buy the chips on my own account through an intermediary and smuggle them into East Germany."

"I thought you hated the Communists," Yount said.

"I did and I still do, more than ever. Don't tell me it was stupid to buy in my own name rather than as an agent; I had no choice. But I did nothing to hurt my country. I handled only eight-bit chips, the kind you can find in any home computer. The commercial attaché said he was doing the business on his own, to save duties. Crooked dealings by Communist officials are not unknown."

"You hid them in your export machinery?" Delmore asked.

"With my own hands. There is plenty of room and a lot of chips fit into a very small space."

"It was a great relief to you that Brundage was killed, wasn't it?" Isabel asked.

Janos looked straight into Isabel's eyes. "I am sure we all have equally interesting stories to tell, Miss Macintosh—even, possibly, Giles Sullivan."

"I do indeed," Giles said, "and I will tell my story equally candidly if a Harvey Brundage puzzle appears that describes my sins. I'm sorry, Janos, that you had to be subjected to this interrogation. We will all, I'm afraid, have to go through the same process if we are to find the murderer and save the rest of us from harm and humiliation. I have one more question to ask, Janos. Do you have access to cyanide?"

Janos looked around. "Does anyone here have a cigarette?" He reached into his jacket pocket, then stopped the motion in disgust. "I threw it away last night. I figured, with Harvey gone, I wouldn't need it anymore, but right now I must have a cigarette, holder or no holder. Cancer is the least of my worries."

"You can get one at the desk in a minute, Janny," Giles said, "although I hope you won't. Just answer my question."

"Sure I can get cyanide," Janos said. "Anyone who deals in machinery can get it. Cyanide is used for case-hardening steel and, to make it worse, in mining precious metals a cyanide solution is used to separate gold and silver from the base metals. So it looks real great for me, doesn't it? But if you have any brains at all, anyone can get cyanide with very little trouble. Ask Delmore if it isn't available in photographic chemicals, for example. Or ask Caroline to look in her encyclopedias. These days you can get instructions on how to build an atom bomb in your basement."

"Please cool down, Janny," Giles said. "You get excited too easily. It's bad for your heart. I'm not accusing you of anything. I don't enjoy this any more than you do, but it has to be done."

"I noticed," Isabel said, "that Lila didn't join in questioning Janos, probably because she knew she would be next. I think you will find that she won't be treated any more leniently than you were. If you stay in your present state of tension, and if you start smoking again, you won't have a chance at even a third prize. So please, Janny, relax. If you're not the killer, this is the only way to make sure your secret is safe."

Janos ran his fingers through his sweat-soaked hair. "I guess you're right, Isabel. I'll pass up the cigarette. It will relax me to have someone else in the hot seat for a change."

13

"So," said Giles, "we come to the Internal Revenue Service. 'TAXTIME,' 'WITHHOLDING,' and 'EVASIVENESS.' Do you want to tell us about it, Lila?"

"Not really," Lila said, "but I guess I have to." She paused to gather her thoughts. "It wasn't a decision. I just sort of slipped into it. Three weeks after Irwin, may he rest in peace, passed away... The accountant handled the sale of the drugstore, which brought much less than Irwin said it was worth, and the insurance... We had so many loans.... After the funeral there was very little left."

"There are many opportunities for a woman with your talents," Yount said. "I wish I had someone like you on my staff."

"A woman in her fifties," Lila said, "with a B.A. in liberal arts? Who never had a job in her life other than to help out in the store after the kids were grown? Believe me, Vergil, if there was anything out there, I would have grabbed it."

"If you had no income," Isabel said, "why worry about the I.R.S.?"

"I started having income that day. It was in the community center. I was always a good Scrabble player, and the guy I was playing was a sore loser, and to a woman yet, which really bothered him. So he kept noodging me I was playing too slow. That's when I invented blitz-Scrabble."

"I didn't know you were the one," Delmore said. "Congratulations."

"Thanks. That and a nickel... Well, I made up the rules right then and there: Ten seconds from the time his last letter goes on the board, your first letter goes down or you've lost the game and an extra hundred points. You have one second to place each letter in your word, and once a letter is placed, you can't shift it. Simple. And because this wise guy had such a big mouth, I bet him a penny a point. I made two bucks that first game and almost ten bucks that day."

"That's how your life of crime started?" Isabel smiled.

"Don't laugh. I went home and thought it over. Big money there wasn't in a community center, but I kept going there for another week. Each day I made eating money. Like clockwork. I discovered that I was fast, really fast, and that I didn't need a lot of time if I trusted my instincts. The next step was to go where I could play for nickels instead of pennies."

"So you came here?" Vergil asked.

"Here I play for dollars. With the quality of competition in this club, nobody beats *anybody* by a hundred points. I went to a slightly more affluent neighborhood community house. Then I found a still richer neighborhood and finally ended up here."

"You were already a crossword whiz when you came here, Lila," Norbert said.

"I didn't play Scrabble all day long, so I did crosswords. After a while I constructed crosswords. The money

67

is lousy, but every little bit helps. Also, I gave classes at the Y. Crosswords are a real godsend to lonely old ladies, and I picked up a few bucks here and there."

"None of which you reported?" Giles asked.

"I reported the checks, all right. Short form. But who keeps count of every little penny you pick up at odd times?"

"Harvey's spies did," Caroline volunteered.

"Yeah, they must have been following me around for a year, recording everything, probably pictures and tapes too. What it must have cost him you shouldn't know from."

"Brundage was a very rich man," Giles said, "and he wanted, very badly, to excel at something, to be respected and admired for some personal attribute."

"For blackmail?" Caroline asked.

"Only we knew it was blackmail," Giles said. "To his friends and to the rest of the world he would have been a champion. I gather from his letter and from our discussions today that Brundage told you all that he was to be the winner in both contests or else?"

"He phoned us each during the week," Norbert said.

"And you thought it best to keep it from me, thinking it would make you look less suspicious?"

"That's about the way it was," Yount said. "We panicked."

"I won't have any more of this," Giles said. "Either you trust me or relieve me of my duties."

"Don't get so stiff, Giles," Lila said. "Can't you see we're baring our souls?"

"Not fully, I'm sure, but I'm used to that. However, if I ask for information directly, I want it to be forthcoming. Is that understood?" There were nods all around. Giles returned to Lila. "I take it, if the I.R.S. were to be informed of your earnings over the past seven years, you'd find it impossible to pay what you owed?"

"With penalties and interest, not in my lifetime. But that isn't the worst part. The I.R.S. is very bad, vindictive. I know. Irwin had a friend once.... They'll clean out your bank account, take all your assets, anything they can get their hands on, and *then* they'll put you in jail as an example. I'm too old to go to jail, Giles."

"What about your children?" Janos asked. "Can't they help you?"

"They're starting out in life and need every penny. I even have to send—I lend them a few dollars now and then."

"What would you do with the prize money if you won?" Isabel asked.

"If I won a first prize—second wouldn't be enough to make a difference—I'd hire a lawyer to make a deal with the I.R.S.; give them the whole prize and declare all my income from now on if they would wash out my past. Naturally, I would be in Canada first with all my money. As Vergil said before, I can make a living anywhere, and my children and grandchildren can visit me in Canada as easily as in New York."

"Why bother going to Canada, then?" Isabel asked.

"I feel a lot safer where the I.R.S. can't get their hot little hands on me or on the prize money. It might make them a little more amenable to making a deal if I'm out of reach."

"You seem to have everything well thought out," Giles said.

"Crosswords I do instinctively; life is a little more complicated. If you're hinting I could have figured out how to kill the creep without anyone knowing, remember, I'm not the only smart one here."

"Would you have any difficulty obtaining cyanide, Lila?"

"I don't know."

"That's an odd answer, Lila. Can you be more explicit?"

"Irwin kept a lot of chemicals in the basement, practically a whole laboratory. Every time he got something in the store, he took home a sample. To experiment with, to invent something to make us rich. Once it was a hair grower; another time it was a depilatory. Irwin was very ambitious. So tonight, when I go home, I'll go through the whole basement. If I find any cyanide, it goes right into the toilet."

"I would leave it alone," Giles said. "If the police find a bottle of cyanide covered with dust, that would be better than a newly cleaned laboratory."

"Dust? In my house? If the police come, they'll find a bottle that's *shining*. With my luck, it'll have my fingerprints on the cap."

 **14**

"THANK YOU FOR BRINGING ME UP-TO-DATE, SIR,"
Oliver said. "I find it a most fascinating case, fully equal
to the best of the British Golden Age of Crime. But if you
will forgive me, sir, I don't think it would be fitting to sit
down with you and Miss Macintosh in the drawing room."

"Don't be such a fusspot, Oliver," Isabel said. "This
isn't Master and Man, this is the interrogation of the Most
Likely Suspect by the Hard-Boiled Dick and His Moll."

"In that case, Miss Macintosh, I will have an Armagnac
and you and your henchman must drink the rotgut. From
the bottle, I'm afraid; this establishment does not have
the proper crystal for cheap Scotch."

"This is serious, Oliver," Isabel said. "If I can't pin
this on you, then Giles and I become the prime suspects."

"There is always Ping, madame. He will gladly confess
when I inform him that American prisons permit television in the cells."

"Unfortunately, Ping had no way of controlling who
got which fish, Oliver."

"A good point, madame. Very well, now that I am
trapped I must reveal all. But would it not look better if,

when I sign the confession, I am in possession of a few more details?"

"Such as?"

"Did I apply the poison in liquid or solid form? Did I sprinkle it on the trout, the potatoes, or the salsify? Was it in a bottle, a box, a spill of paper, or compressed into a pill? With which hand did I apply the poison, the one holding the plate or the one holding the server? When did—"

"Oh, my God," Giles said. "We don't know anything. I feel like a complete amateur."

"You *are* a complete amateur, sir," Oliver said. "As a private eye, you are not fit to blacken Ellery Queen's shoes. Even Miss Marple, if you will forgive my saying so, could teach you step one. But I do have faith in your ability to learn quickly and well, under the proper tutelage and given the proper incentive." He took the big gold watch from his vest, snapped open the lid, and said, "I arranged for your brother, Mr. Percival, to take your call at this very moment, sir. Permit me to turn on the speaker so that Miss Macintosh may share the information."

"And you, too, Oliver?"

"I find it easier," Oliver said, dialing the number, "and less irritating to you, sir, to listen in on the pantry phone. But if you insist, sir, I will remain to provide such services as you may require." He spoke into the phone. "Mr. Sullivan? Oliver here. Mr. Giles requires your assistance."

"Your finger broke, Giles?" came the rough loud voice over the speaker. "Can't call your own brother direct?"

"It's just Oliver's way of putting me in my place, Percival. Isabel Macintosh is present and you're on the speaker, so mind your language."

"She's the head of a co-ed school, ain't she? I'll bet she knows words I never even heard of."

"I do, Percival," Isabel said, "and if you're a good boy I'll write them down for you to study. The only problem is, who's going to read them to you?"

"Ha, you got a good one there, Giles. Why don't you propose, like a decent man should, before she finds out what a stuffed shirt you are?"

"I can't even handle Oliver," Giles said, "and now I've got three of you needling me. I need information, Percival. Badly. Do you know what's going on?"

"Of course I do. Lieutenant Faber called me this morning—they still remember the old man—gave me everything we had. Wanted my help in putting you away where you can't poison any more arbitragers or bring other shame on the good name of Sullivan."

"It was cyanide, wasn't it?"

"Potassium cyanide, powdered, in a gelatin capsule. As soon as Brundage bit down on it, he was a dead man."

"Wouldn't he have noticed the shape and texture of a capsule?"

"With a mouthful of trout, potatoes, and vegetables? And the toasted almonds? He didn't; that's for sure. The almonds are crunchy, and about the same size and shape."

"That clinches it; whoever did it knew we would be having trout amandine."

"Brilliant, Giles. Keep up the good work and soon you'll be allowed to carry a genuine magnifying glass. Of course it was one of you guys. By the way, where is *your* cyanide pellet? The one you took home from the war?"

"I turned it in."

"Pull the other one, Giles; this is me you're talking to."

"Besides, a pill is not a capsule."

"Even a bigshot lawyer can figure out how to crush a pill into powder and slip it in a capsule. Why don't you confess Giles? Faber needs to win a big one so he can get a leg up on a promotion."

"I didn't have any motive to kill Brundage."

"That anyone knows of, you mean. If I sweated you, without a fancy lawyer hanging around, you'd sing."

"If I did dislike him, why should I kill him in my own home while I was sitting next to him?"

"Nobody ever accused you of being smart, Giles, just intelligent. You could have been a cop, you know; Pop would have liked that. But you had to pick the other side of the fence."

"Lawyers are not against the police, Percival."

"Sure they are, Giles, especially criminal lawyers. You had your chance to carry on the way Pop wanted, and you muffed it. I hope you're happy. Maybe it's better you didn't; you'd have been a lousy cop. Now what do you want? I've got a bowling date."

"That was forty years ago, Percy; can't you ever forget?"

"Never. Speak up or hang up."

"Please keep me informed, Percy. Any new evidence, new information, whatever the police get. I have to find the killer, fast."

"You finally joined the good guys, Giles? Now that your own neck is on the line, you want to play cops and robbers?"

"Don't do this to me, Percy; I'm serious."

"What'll you do if I help you get him, Giles? Offer him your services? Get him off on a technicality? For a big fee?"

"I'm trying to save some innocent—some people who don't deserve to be hurt, Percy. That's all."

"What about all the killers you put back on the street, Giles? *They* didn't kill some innocent people? Before and *after* the trial? One of them was a cop, remember? Four kids?"

"There's no point rehashing everything, Percy. I upheld the law, same as you. Right now I need your help. Either you give it or you don't. You decide. And whether you do or not, I'm still going after the killer."

"*You* upheld the law; I upheld justice. There's a difference, Giles. Oh, I'll help you, all right, out of respect for the name of Sullivan and in memory of my big brother, the one I used to look up to when I was a kid. But if you catch the killer, just remember, I'll be watching. Just to see what you do with him *after* you catch him." The phone banged down hard.

Giles sat staring straight ahead. Isabel walked over to him and held his hand against her breast.

Oliver put a snifter in front of Giles and poured in an inch of brandy, then, judiciously, added another inch. "Now that you are no longer the Tough Private Eye, sir, you may drink like a gentleman again. When you are finished, I have some more news for you."

━━━━━━━━━━━━━━━━━━━━━━━━━ **15** ━━━

SULLIVAN PUT DOWN HIS BRANDY SNIFTER. SATISFIED that he was calm again, Oliver said, "Your friend from Washington, sir, Mr. Barker. He called just before you came home this evening."

Giles looked sharply at Oliver, then glanced at Isabel. "It's quite all right, sir. You don't have to call him back."

"What did he say, Oliver?"

"He inquired after your health, sir, having heard you were ill. I assured him it was only a slight upper respiratory infection and that you would soon be better."

"Was that all?"

"He asked if you required antibiotics. I told him I did not think it necessary. He said to tell you that if there was anything else you needed, you could always reach him at home."

"Thank you, Oliver," Giles said. "Let's call it a day."

"Not yet, Giles," Isabel said. "We have to talk about the murder. Early tomorrow morning we'll have another crossword puzzle to solve, and two more interrogations based on what the crossword says. Please stay, Oliver; we need your unique way of looking at things."

"One does one's best, Miss Macintosh." Clearly

pleased, he poured himself another brandy.

"I'm still concerned," Isabel said, "about the possibility that the killer may do it again. We started to discuss it before and dropped the matter without coming to a conclusion."

"If a second murder is committed," Oliver said, "it greatly increases the chances the killer will be apprehended."

"If a second murder is committed," Isabel said, "it greatly decreases my chances for a happy life. I don't have all that many good friends, you know. Of either sex."

"Me?" Giles was puzzled. "I'm just an innocent bystander."

"That in itself, darling, increases the odds. Read the papers. But the real reason is that you're the only one who has a chance to find the killer. And he knows it."

"I'm not a detective."

"You know that, Giles, and I know that, and Oliver can *prove* it beyond a reasonable doubt, but put yourself in the killer's shoes. You're a criminal lawyer, a spy, and, for a man, very bright."

"I'm an *ex*–criminal lawyer, Isabel, and all I did in the war was a little cryptography. Norbert Kantor is more intelligent than me and thee put together, and you can throw in Oliver for good measure. I'm the wrong person for the job; I shouldn't have volunteered."

"You tell him, Oliver. I might not say it as gracefully."

"The word Miss Macintosh was looking for, sir, is, I am afraid, bullshit, if you will forgive the expression." Isabel nodded. "If Mr. Kantor, with all due respect, sir, were to be eliminated, the investigation would proceed apace, probably with an even greater chance of success. Not only would the number of suspects be decreased, thus narrowing the choices, but the second crime, juxtaposed with the first, might provide additional clues that would seal the doom of the killer."

"You seem very knowledgeable about all this, Oliver," Isabel said.

"I read a great deal, Miss Macintosh, and I have, I am sure, the largest collection of classical whodunits, from Conan Doyle to Resnicow, of all the butlers in the United States and, possibly, in the English-speaking world." He paused. "To return to the matter at hand, sir, while you do not have the intelligence of Mr. Kantor, the quickness of Mrs. Quinn, the intestinal fortitude of Mr. Miklosz, the youth of Mr. Rankin, the encyclopedic knowledge of Miss Trimble, or the influence of Mr. Yount—"

"It's true, then," Giles interrupted, "the old saying that no man is a hero to his butler, but do you have to be so specific?"

"The saying, sir, is that no man is a hero to his valet, so possibly we should add to the list that you are not as well read in the classics as one would like. Nevertheless, you do have all the elements I noted in a high degree, in a combination that makes you the only person involved in this case who could possibly solve the puzzle."

"And you have me, darling," Isabel said. "I have talents you couldn't possibly imagine."

"And which I'm afraid to ask about."

"You may count on my support, too, sir, should violence be unavoidable."

"You're both crazy," Giles said. "There will be no violence, and we can't possibly find the killer by Sunday night. If Brundage follows the pattern he started, we won't even have the third puzzle until Saturday morning."

"The flash of insight, sir, that all great fictional detectives have just before the dénouement comes in a brief second, once all the elements have been assembled, usually the day before all the suspects are gathered together in a drawing room."

"For flashes of insight you need Lila Quinn, not me."

"Lila is a suspect, Giles. If she did it, she'll try to confuse us."

"They'll all try to confuse us, Isabel. Do you really think that Janny and Lila told us the whole truth this morning?"

"See? You're acting like a detective already. You're a natural."

"I have no choice, with both of you against me. All right, then. Oliver, did you notice anyone reaching toward Harvey Brundage's plate?"

"No, sir, and I was observing very closely, to make sure the glasses were filled and that everyone had what was needed."

"How about when you were serving the fish? Did anyone make a motion that would have allowed him to put a capsule on the trout served to Harvey?"

"No, sir. The serving platter was behind and to the left of each person, and I had my eyes on it all the time. Further, the fish were not laid out in a line. Even I did not know which fish Mr. Brundage would get."

"The potatoes, or the salsify, then. Was it possible?"

"I'd stake my life on it, sir; no one could have put anything into the food while I was serving without my noticing."

"What about before serving?" Isabel asked. "While the plates were empty?"

Oliver thought for a moment. "That is possible, Miss Macintosh. I did not watch the empty plates. My eyes are not as sharp as they once were, and I might not have noticed a small white capsule against the white china if my attention were fixed on serving properly. Mashed potatoes can drip, salsify is slippery, trout is unwieldy, and it is important that each person gets a large, satisfactory portion of toasted almonds."

"Harvey could have had his attention distracted," Isabel said, "for that minute or so between the time the capsule was placed on his plate and the time Oliver served the potatoes."

"We were talking," Giles said, "so none of us was looking at plates. Did you see anything, Oliver?"

"No, sir, but when Ping rolled in the hot tray, all eyes, including mine, were fixed on him. Anyone could have put a *bottleful* of poison on anyone else's plate at that time and I would not have seen it. Misdirection, the magicians call it."

"Actually," Isabel said, "it would have been easiest for you, Giles, or for me. Janos would have had to reach across me, and Vergil across you, to get to Harvey's plate. Delmore and Norbert would have had an even harder job. For Caroline or Lila it would have been impossible."

"Didn't both Caroline and Lila get up from their places during the meal?"

"Caroline did, I'm sure. I think it was after the soup. I don't remember Lila. I was talking to Janos when I wasn't actually eating, sort of turned to him a little. I didn't want to talk to Harvey; something about him bothered me."

"So the conclusion is, Giles, that whoever put the poison in Harvey's plate did it in full sight of all the people at the table and, by misdirection, made sure no one saw him."

"Not necessarily, Miss Macintosh," Oliver said.

"But if someone saw—Oh, I see. Someone did see him do it and decided to keep his mouth shut. Because the witness also wanted Harvey dead."

"Or saw an opportunity, Miss Macintosh, to follow Mr. Brundage's example—to blackmail the killer."

"Wouldn't the witness have jumped, or acted surprised, for a moment?" Giles asked.

"Not necessarily, sir. Your colleagues are all rather quick-witted people. But there is still another option, sir. *Murder on the Orient Express*."

"They all did it, Oliver?"

"Collaborated, sir. Not necessarily all, but most. It is a logical conclusion that satisfies all the requirements."

"No, Oliver. Norbert Kantor, for one, would not do anything immoral. Nor Caroline Trimble."

"May I remind you, sir, that Mr. Kantor, upright as he is, and Miss Trimble, timid as she appears, have already done something for which each can be blackmailed and that if made public could destroy their lives."

"You have a point there, Oliver. And you've just shown me how impossible this case is."

"Maybe tomorrow's puzzle will make things clearer, darling," Isabel said. "Let's go to bed."

"But it's only nine o'clock," Giles protested.

Isabel looked at him pityingly. "And you call yourself a detective?"

16

"**A**NYONE BUT ME TODAY, GOD. PLEASE," DELMORE said.

"Still hoping the messenger falls off his bike," Vergil said, "and the puzzles go down a sewer?"

"Or a cyclone dumps them into Oz," Delmore said. "I'll take anything that works."

"Did it ever occur to you," Norbert said, "that if we miss a puzzle, we may never find the murderer? Which means that next week we might as well leave the country."

"That's next week," Delmore said. "Right now, day-to-day is all I can handle."

"We've got two Canadas and a Brazil," Isabel said. "Where are you planning to run away to next Tuesday, Norbert?"

"Israel. I'd love to be a librarian on a kibbutz."

"Kibbutzim don't need librarians," Lila said. "They need strong backs and weak minds to pull weeds from the onion fields."

"What's the difference?" Norbert said. "If I don't win a prize, I couldn't afford the air fare anyway."

"I'm sure they'd love to have you at one of the universities," Janos said.

"Sure. Next school year, a year and a half away. Who takes care of my family meanwhile? Welfare?"

"This is terrible," Caroline whispered. "Lila's going to Canada, Norbert's going to Israel, Janny's going to Costa Rica, probably. What about people who can't go away? Are we giving up finding the murderer?"

"No, Caroline," Giles said, "but I can understand their feelings. It makes sense to plan for the worst, but we won't give up. In fact, we haven't really started."

"When *will* we start, Giles?" Vergil asked. "After we solve the third puzzle? That's Saturday morning. The solvers contest is Saturday night."

"He's right," Delmore said. "You explained why we have to find the murderer before the prizes are given out at the awards ceremony dinner. That's Sunday night. How are you going to find the killer in a day and a half?"

"I get all the information the police have, all the leads, almost as soon as they get them."

"You have a spy in the police force?" Vergil asked.

"My brother, Percival, still has lots of friends there, men he helped when he was chief of detectives."

"You don't tell your brother what we tell you, I hope," Lila said, looking worried.

"Certainly not," Giles said, "and I never would."

"Have you come up with anything yet?" Norbert asked.

"Well." Giles paused uncomfortably. "I don't think Oliver did it."

"Great," Lila said. "And if we're real lucky, by tonight you'll eliminate Ping?"

"There's no need to be sarcastic, Lila," Giles said. "Not everybody has ESP. The police haven't done any better, you know."

"That's a relief," Lila said. "For a moment I was afraid they were going to beat us to it."

ACROSS

1 The man's
4 Flower or tree
9 States of depression
14 Turkish title
15 Vaudeville show
16 "___ hooks"
17 Diploma indication
19 Absorbent cloth
20 Aweigh
21 Three: prefix
23 Envision
24 One who blows a horn
26 Elizabeth's husband
28 South American beast
30 Buccaneer
33 Encrust
36 Pleasures
38 Very short putt
39 Egg: prefix
40 Fudge
42 Self
43 Individualist
45 Girl's toy
46 Ship's workers
47 Contemporaries of the Saxons
49 Signal light
51 Me
53 "Wait Till the Sun Shines, ___"
57 Undergarment
59 What horses eat
60 Uninteresting
61 Hemp fiber used as a caulk
63 Repeated wrongly
67 Sphere of action
68 Approximately
69 Upon: prefix
70 Broadcast again
71 Complications
72 Highway: abbr.

DOWN

1 Attacked
2 "___ prepare a place . . .": John 14:2
3 Pelvic vertebrae: prefix
4 Drive forward
5 Celtic sea god
6 Actress Gardner
7 Pecan or cashew
8 Molars
9 Uselessness
10 G.I. entertainment org.
11 Daily purchase
12 Patellar area
13 Only
18 Name
22 Tear
25 Hindu prince
26 What persistence does
27 A Gershwin
29 Type of fungus
31 Buster Brown's dog
32 Sufficient: archaic
33 Soft-drink flavor
34 Shakespeare's river
35 Checkers player, ultimately
37 Window frame part
40 First-year collegian
41 Filled pastry
44 English cathedral town
46 String instrument
48 Ocean
50 Contradicts
52 1970s outfielder Bostock
54 Subsequently
55 Clumsy
56 Jockey Arcaro
57 Swine
58 Scarce
62 Actress Merkel
64 Nigerian language
65 Turf
66 What: Spanish

UNETHICAL

Fredericks opened the door of the conference room and without a word placed the eight puzzles on the table. By the time the door had closed behind him, Lila and Janos had completed the first line Across.

 **17**

"THIRTY-FIVE DOWN IS CUTE," LILA SAID. "BUT FIFTY-seven Across; some editors wouldn't allow that."

"They have to be careful," Caroline said. "You never know who does the puzzle."

"I still can't believe you beat Lila on a conventional," Delmore said.

"I just did the Acrosses," Janos admitted, "and didn't worry about mistakes; those I can correct later. In the contest I'll be more careful."

"Do me a favor, Janny," Lila said, "and break a finger. You know I need a first in the solvers to square myself with Internal Revenue. There's no way I can beat you or Norbert in constructing."

"I need the money, too, Lila," Janos said. "There's no way a man my age can start fresh in a foreign country without any money. I love you all, but me first; you second."

"Don't you dare start that again," Isabel said. "You people are all crazy, do you know that? Here we are, an impossible task with an impossible deadline, and all you can think about is the quality of the puzzle. The analysis of the motives, the characters, of each of you is the only path toward finding the murderer. These puzzles are the tools, the wedges, to crack open the shells you're all hiding inside of. None of you would say a word if we didn't have the puzzles; you're all too busy thinking of ways to skip the country before Wednesday. Now, start analyzing the words or, by God, I'll take Giles to Vermont and leave you all here to stew in your own juices."

"Don't be so hard on us, Isabel," Delmore said. "Everything you said is true. We *know* you're right, but still . . . I don't really want—none of us does—to tell you about—anything. I guess I will—I'll have to, and maybe it's even good for me—but I want to put off taking the bitter medicine as long as possible. That doesn't make me crazy, Isabel. Only human."

"And besides," Caroline said, "this puzzle isn't as easy to analyze as the first one. *Unethical* is much harder to pin down than *Illegal*. There aren't all that many combinations of words that make sense. The only one I see offhand is 'AGA,' 'HADAT,' and 'RAJA.' Maybe there's an Indian prince named Hadat who was robbed—the 'Eye of the Idol' story?"

"That would be illegal, not unethical," Norbert said.

"If the robber were in a position of trust . . . ?"

"Forget it, Caroline," Lila said. "None of us could ever have been close enough to an Indian prince to . . . I like 'PIRATE,' 'ATRIP,' and 'CREW.' That's a ship being hijacked. Or maybe a mutiny. Anyone here take a sea voyage recently? And 'OAKUM'—that's used for caulking the seams in a boat. 'PROPEL' could be the propeller."

"Two other words, 'KNEE' and 'SOLE,' fit with 'ATRIP' better," Caroline said. "Something bad might have happened on a walking trip. And 'KNEE' appeared in yesterday's puzzle too. Harvey has to be trying to tell us something."

"'KNEE' fits better with three other words," Vergil said. 'IRA,' 'SOD,' and 'ARENA.' 'IRA' is the Irish Republican Army, of course. Ireland is called the Old Sod by all wearers o' the green. And the 'ARENA' is Northern Ireland. The IRA is known for shooting off the kneecaps of informers."

"No one here is of Irish descent," Janos said.

"Sullivan is not quite a Jewish name," said Lila.

There was an uncomfortable silence before Isabel spoke. "I'm telling you for the last time," she said, "leave Giles out of this. If he gets sore at you, or worse, if I get sore at you for him . . ."

"If I have to suffer through this," Vergil said, "Giles must suffer too. No one's in the clear yet, Isabel. Giles himself said that if his secrets come up in a puzzle, he'll tell us about them. So don't threaten us. One hour after any one of us pulls out, I'm on my way to someplace else. I don't want to go, but I will if I have to. So let's forget the prima donna scene and get back to work. Okay?" He looked around and, satisfied, said, "Okay."

"Right," Janos said. "I see a possible. 'COLA,' 'RIP,' and 'PLANT.' If we take 'COLA' as representing coca, which is the plant from which cocaine is derived, and 'RIP' to be short for ripoff, or theft, someone here stole cocaine. 'PLANT' could even be the laboratory where the cocaine was manufactured and from which it was stolen."

"I have something more likely," Norbert said. "'RARE,' 'SACRO,' and 'FALSIFY.' Someone forged a sacred book, a rare sacred book. And 'LLAMA,' that could be the closest Brundage could get to 'lama.' It has to be a

Tibetan sacred book, a four-word fit. And we're all word people. Perfect. Caroline, do you have any recollection of a costly, rare Tibetan sacred book being auctioned off within the last few years?"

"Something terrible just occurred to me," Caroline said. "What will happen when—if—these puzzles are printed in the newspapers next Wednesday? In just two puzzles we've discovered twenty crimes, and we were looking for words to make three- or four-word patterns. When fifty million crossword fans start looking... My God, they'll find... I'm sure some of them will look for two-word combinations. Or even one word. There isn't a word in the English language you can't fit into a crime, and that includes *the*. They'll think we're the center of crime for the whole world. Our reputations—"

"They'll think the Cruciverbal Club is the center," Vergil said. "Because we're the board of directors. Every member will be tarred with the same brush. We'll be lucky if the good citizens don't bomb the place with us inside."

"We'd better do something fast," Delmore said.

"Like find the killer?" Lila said sarcastically. "*Now* you have a reason; before you didn't?"

"At least let's get the puzzle solved," Delmore said.

"The puzzle is solved," Norbert said. "Its meaning is the problem."

"We're not doing it right," Lila said. "I tried that sideways look Isabel told us about yesterday and nothing jumped out. The creep got more subtle in this one. Maybe if we looked for *who* it is rather than—'DOCTOR-ATE,'" he said triumphantly, "that's the key. There are two doctorates here, Norbert and Giles. Let's see what else fits. Of course. 'FALSIFY' and 'MISQUOTED.' Hmmmm. That could fit both of you. It would be a waste of time to ask Giles; lawyers lie very easily." She stared directly at Kantor. "Is it you, Norbert?"

He looked back at her for a moment, then dropped his eyes. "I didn't remember," he said guiltily. "It's been— such a shock. I thought . . . I was sure that I . . . It never occurred to me; I had really forgotten all about it. I never even thought that I could be capable of doing something unethical."

"I see the other one," Delmore said suddenly. "If the key is occupations, then the clues are 'NEWSPAPER,' 'PAYSOFF,' and 'KINGMAKER.' Vergil Yount."

"I guess that's me, all right," Yount said. "I had glossed over the 'NEWSPAPER.' I'm a columnist, a political commentator, not a newspaperman. And I never considered myself a kingmaker. The reason I didn't put it all together was 'PAYSOFF.' I never took a payoff in my life; I swear it. But now that I see it all together, I can understand. . . ." Tears formed in his eyes. "It's the end of—everything. Not just for me; for you, too, all of you. For everybody, all over the world. And it could have been so . . . It really could."

"Would you like me to get you a drink?" Delmore asked.

"Thanks, Del, but I don't think it will help. Nothing can help me now." Vergil sat silent for a while, looking down. Then he spoke. "You know, all my adult life I've been surrounded by politicians. I hated them, really hated them. I hadn't met one I would invite into my home, or would even want to be seen in public with socially. Some were stupid, just plain stupid, and the rest were totally self-serving or outright crooked. I never met one who would come out of Washington, or a statehouse, poorer than when he went in. Not all of them took money; some took favors: sex, liquor, stock tips, legal fees, government contracts. Hell, there wasn't one of them couldn't be bought with *something*. And any of them, *all* of them, would sell their souls for a hundred-vote plurality."

"Not all, evidently," Isabel said.

"Not all," Vergil agreed. "So when the Senator came up, I didn't believe it. I was sure, positive, that someplace, somehow, he had found a new way to steal. So I kept a special eye on him. But he wasn't stealing or whoring or drinking or lining up a big job somewhere, or anything. When he was taken out, he didn't order alfalfa sprouts on organic pita for show, or a tin of Malossol out of greed. He ordered what he usually ate and he watched the right side of the menu too."

"Sounds too good to be true," Lila said. "Has to be a catch."

"That's what I thought. But after a while I became a believer. Then I watched him on the floor. He went with the party most of the time—why not? That's why he joined in the first place. But when it was something he felt strongly about, he spoke up, he fought, and he voted the way he thought was right. He made some enemies, some friends, and began to be respected. He wasn't stupid, either. Not that he was a real brain, like you guys, but he was head and shoulders above the yo-yos around him."

"Isn't that a handicap for a politician?" Isabel asked. "Intelligence, I mean? Look how it hurt Adlai Stevenson."

"He didn't flaunt it and he wasn't highly miseducated; he just had the right gut instincts. He understood what he was doing *after* he decided what was right. Here was a *real* liberal, I figured, not a *talk-gooder* or one of those cold doctrinaires who'll donate *your* life to push *their* pet ideologies."

"I heard that your columns were the deciding factor,"

Giles said, "in getting him a second term."

"I like to think so, just as I think it was me . . . A few words once in a while in my column and a man becomes important, sought after. He gets on major committees; his good works come to the public eye and to the party chiefs. It snowballs. Right now he's a shoo-in for a third term. After that . . . we deserve a president of that caliber."

"So if it weren't for the money . . ." Isabel said.

"Exactly. I make a lot of money. I spend a lot of money. I have lots of obligations. I drink too much, and I'm often broke. So one day I'm sitting with the Senator's senior staff man in a quiet bar. He's tipping me off on an important bill coming up in a major committee, a whole column's worth of news. When we're finished—they don't take credit cards there—I find I can't pay the check. No problem, he pays. And seeing my face, he discreetly slips me a few bills. Nothing intended. He's a good guy; I'll pay him back next time I see him."

"But you didn't," Delmore said.

"A coincidence. I had money with me for a week, plenty. But by the time I meet him, I'm flat again. So guess what?"

"He lends you a little more," Janos said.

"All very nice. No recriminations. I'm half-soused, so I don't have sense enough to refuse. Somehow this keeps going until, by now, I'm dependent on it, couldn't live without it. It's like pennies from heaven, tax-free. Every week."

"Where does he get the money?" Giles asked.

"He's not rich, so it's not from his salary. It must be from the Senator's election funds. Which means he has to sign for it. Nobody questions him; he's trusted but the signatures are there. Regular. If there were an audit—

and you never know—he hangs. He hangs, I hang, the Senator hangs, the country hangs, everybody. Brundage found it; any good investigator could."

"Couldn't you . . . ?" Caroline asked. "The truth?"

"What's the truth? If I had these facts in front of me, this evidence, I'd write a column, a week's worth of columns, that would have the guy's own mother screaming for his blood."

"So you need to win a prize badly," Lila said.

"Both prizes." The words were clipped short. "So the money could go back quickly. Or else, time. My agent is negotiating a new fee schedule. I told her to take a thousand a week and put it into an account I can't touch. I put in; somebody else takes out."

"But even if you win both first prizes," Giles said, "you can't protect yourself, or the Senator, if the facts hit the papers next Wednesday."

"As of Monday morning I intend to be out of the country on a fact-finding trip until after Wednesday. There's no way the money can be put back if people are watching. My friend needs time and privacy to do things right. Brundage outsmarted the killer. My only hope now is that you find him fast."

"And if you're the killer, Vergil?" Lila asked.

"I'd do exactly the same thing I'm doing now, so what's the difference? You can't tell if I or any of us is the killer by the way we try to protect ourselves. So don't go reading anything into my actions that isn't there."

"I have to, Vergil," Giles said softly. "I am judge and I'm jury and, in effect, executioner. I have to work with what I have, which is your actions and your words, nothing else. You're my friends, all my friends, yet I must hunt, kill, one of you to save the rest. Do justice, my brother says; within the law, say I. I have little chance of winning, and I dare not leave the game."

"Let's take a break," Lila said. "I have to phone my travel agent."

18

"ARE YOU READY TO TALK NOW, NORBERT?" GILES asked when they had all seated themselves. "Are you able to talk?"

"I'm ready," Kantor said, "and I'm able, but I'm not so sure I'm willing." He smiled wanly at the weak joke. "It's a shock to find out about yourself—that you're not what you thought you were, that you've been fooling yourself for all these years."

"The others," Isabel said, "they've all done things they're ashamed of. Did you think you were above that, Norbert?"

He thought for a moment. "I never looked at it that way, but yes, I think I did. I thought if a man tried to live by the Law, the Torah, with all his heart and soul, he could. I thought I had. I fooled only myself. The mind is funny that way. How clearly I can see the mistakes of others, their faults and their transgressions; how blind I became when I looked into my own soul."

"You will feel better," Giles said. "When you confess you will be better."

"Cleansed of my sins?" Kantor smiled. "I cannot be, Giles, I'm not a Catholic. I alone am responsible for my deeds, all my sins, and I alone must bear their burden. God alone can forgive me; I cannot forgive myself."

"We don't have time for a lecture on theology," Lila said. "You're gonna talk? Talk."

"My wife and I," Norbert Kantor said, "were each twenty when we married. I had just entered my Master's program and Claire had taken a job at a day-care center near our apartment. The idea was that I would concentrate on my studies, get my doctorate as quickly as possible, get a job teaching, and then we would have children. Unfortunately, or fortunately, as it turned out, Robbie came one week before I was awarded my Master's.

"Of course, the program I had planned was out. Claire did what she could, typing and other work that could be done at home, but I had to earn the rent money, the food money, and whatever else was needed. I did some tutoring, got a graduate assistantship, taught part-time at a local yeshiva; one way or another, I managed. My doctoral work went into slow gear, but we were very happy, my little family and I.

"Then Claire—God blessed us with another baby. Claire, with two young babies, had very little spare time, so I had to take on additional work: proofreading, copyediting, whatever I could do at home to bring in a few dollars. My thesis slowed down even more.

"We went on like this until we had our third child. Claire had no time for anything but the children and the house. I got a Sunday job as a busboy and stopped all work on my dissertation.

"After three months my thesis adviser told me I had to show progress or he'd be forced to drop me from the program. I might lose my assistantship as well. I had to work on my thesis.

"Claire's mother saved us. We would move into her

apartment, small as it was, until I got my doctorate. She would help Claire with the children, and do the cooking and shopping, so Claire could do some paying work at home. The money we saved on food and rent would enable me to give up one job. My contribution would be to sleep less and to complete my dissertation within one year."

"You did, evidently," Giles said. "Successfully too."

"Oh, yes, I did. It was hard work, but it was good work. I had everything ready one month before the deadline, when the thesis had to go to the binder: notes and quotes, footnotes, annotations, bibliography, statistical data, tables, everything. Handwritten. We had a system set up. I would give each page a final check, Claire would type it, then I would proofread and correct. We figured it could be done in two weeks, leaving two more weeks for emergencies. Then Robbie threw all my interviews and statistical data into the washing machine."

"Oh, God," Caroline said. "I would have died."

"I almost did. Four years of work down the drain. Literally. Even now it gives me chills."

"So you faked everything?" Delmore said.

"My analysis was sound; my conclusions were valid. All I did was to fake the exact quotes of my interviews and questionnaires and to fill in table after table with data that resembled my original data as well as I could remember and that would lead, logically, to my conclusions."

"Couldn't your examiners tell?" Isabel asked.

"How could they? Could they duplicate my interviews, my questionnaires, my word counts, the pages upon pages . . . ? No, they had to trust my data, which was, after all, not far from accurate. My conclusions were not that outlandish. I attacked no one; it was just a new way of observing how words evolved, one that has proven very useful in the field. But the main reason was that there is, implicit in this process, a dependence on the integrity of the candidates which, with very few exceptions, is well justified."

"How could Brundage have found this out?" Janos asked.

"Only one way. My mother-in-law must have said something to one of her friends, and she said something to somebody, and so on, and one of Brundage's investigators picked it up and followed through on it enough to see what happened."

"Can it be proven that your data were inaccurate?" Giles asked.

"If someone wanted to take the trouble."

"What would be the consequences?"

"Other than the shame and the blow to the profession? Next year you'd find me pulling weeds in the onion fields of Israel."

Isabel stood up and looked straight into Kantor's eyes. "Would you kill," she asked, "to protect yourself from humiliation and from losing your job and from leaving your profession?"

"I would kill"—he looked straight back into her eyes—"to protect my wife, my children, my country, and my religion. I would not kill to benefit myself."

"Looked at in one way," Isabel said, "killing Brundage would protect your wife and children. And your friends."

"Looked at another way, Isabel, it would be a self-serving act and against the Commandments."

There was a moment's silence, then Giles said, "Do you have access to cyanide, Norbert?"

"Not directly, Giles. But I have friends in the Chemistry Department. I'm sure, if there is any there, I could get a small amount without anyone noticing it. From what I've learned recently, cyanide isn't easy to get, but if you're determined, it can be gotten."

"You forgot to ask Vergil about the cyanide," Isabel said. She turned to Yount. "Can you get cyanide?"

"I have so many contacts in the C.I.A. that I could get enough cyanide to kill a hundred people. And none of them would talk about it afterward. In fact, they'd fall all over themselves to give me a pill or two, special delivery, with the director's blessing. Can you imagine what it would be worth to the C.I.A. to have a political columnist in its pocket? Or even just owing them a favor? Carrying this to its logical conclusion, they'd consider ten Harvey Brundages a fair trade for one Vergil Yount, columnist supreme, and even throw in a left-hitting outfielder. I wouldn't even have to be in the same city as the victim when he got hit by the truck. So why should I do it myself, the hard way? Chew that one over, Giles."

‖‖‖‖‖‖‖‖‖‖‖‖‖‖‖‖‖‖‖‖‖‖‖‖‖‖‖‖‖‖‖‖ **19** ‖‖‖‖

ISABEL BOUGHT TWO BAGS OF HOT CHESTNUTS AND LED Giles to a park bench. "We're not getting anywhere," she said. "Are we?"

"Of course we are," he said. "Look at all we know about Janos, Lila, Norbert, and Vergil."

"We know they had good reason to kill Brundage, but we knew that before."

"I mean about their characters. Each one reacted in a different way, faced adversity differently, solved the problems differently. Harvey Brundage was a problem. We can figure out which was the most likely to solve the Harvey problem in the way it was solved. When I was practicing law, I would question everyone repeatedly, particularly my client. You'd be surprised at what is revealed if one persists. In the war it was sometimes necessary to question people for days and days. Then, when the stories finally came together, the holes and discrepancies were found and the clues led to the truth."

"We don't have days and days, Giles. The first contest is tomorrow night."

"We'll get another puzzle tomorrow morning. There

will be more information available to us at that time."

"Sure, Giles. It will show that Delmore and Caroline have pasts they would kill to keep secret. Do you have to embarrass them like that?"

"What do we really know about our directors, Isabel? Nice people, intelligent, quick-witted, skilled with words? Certainly. All of that. But did you suspect that each was capable of the kind of crime we heard them admit to yesterday? And today? And will hear tomorrow?"

"There but for the grace of God go I, Giles. And you, too, I'm sure."

"Exactly. Each crime has a direct bearing on that person's potential for murder. From what you've heard so far, which one would you select?"

Isabel didn't hesitate. "Lila Quinn. She's quick, instinctive, acts directly on her decision. And poison is—classically—a woman's weapon."

"So we did learn something from each story. That's why we must continue. Besides, it's the only method we've got."

"Why didn't you ask each one what he saw during the dinner?"

"A waste of time. No one could have seen more than you and I. If anyone had seen anything, we would have known it by now. With the threats they all have hanging over their heads, do you think any one of them would not speak up if he even *suspected* he might have seen something? Do you think that a capsule of cyanide could have been placed on Harvey's plate without one of us, or Oliver, seeing some movement? If *we* didn't see anything, no one else did either."

"So how are we going to find the killer, Giles?"

"By analyzing the personality, the character, of each

suspect. The way you picked Lila. Bad choice, by the way."

"Really, Sullivan? Pray tell why?"

"Because, Macintosh, she was as far from Harvey as Caroline. Because she's a lady, over sixty, and Jewish, to boot."

"*I'm* a lady, Sullivan, and there are times I could kill with pleasure, especially if it's a man who patronizes me. As for her age, I'm well over fifty and I doubt that I'll change my character just because I get a little older. In fact, I like my character just the way it is, and you'd better like it, too, or else. And you can put that Jewish myth to rest, too. Norbert Kantor is *Orthodox* Jewish, and I'd hate to get caught between him and a Nazi who's threatening his wife and kids. As a matter of fact, I hear the Israeli army is full of Jews—quite a few of them wear skullcaps and carry prayer books into battle—and they're supposed to be pretty tough. So why not Lila?"

"My money's on Vergil Yount, Macintosh. Don't let that Southern courtesy fool you, or that fat, alcohol-soaked look. Everybody's seen him drinking, but no one's seen him drunk. He's got a mind like a steel trap, he's a success in a town of back-knifers, and he's never backed down, not even for a president."

"They're all tough, Giles. Have you forgotten Miklosz? What he went through to get where he is? He must be made of steel."

"Delmore isn't tough, Isabel; neither is Caroline. The trouble is, you don't have to be tough to be a murderer. Sometimes a weak person who has had more than he can stand will kill faster than a strong person who has other ways of attacking a bad situation. Some of my clients have been more like Caroline than like Janny."

"I suppose you're right, Giles, which leaves us exactly where we were before. Any of them could be the killer, and we have no evidence yet that shows which one."

"Something will come out tomorrow, Isabel."

"You hope. Why don't you call your brother, see if the police have found anything new?"

"He'll call me if they have, just to rub my face in it."

"He loves you, Giles, and he's proud of you. I can tell."

"He has a funny way of showing it."

"What do you want him to do, Giles? Kiss you in public?"

"Why not? Yes. Figuratively. Tell me in front of another cop that he's proud of me."

"I think he'd like to do that, Giles. Meet him halfway."

"How?"

"Phone him. Better yet, visit him with me, to thank him for the help he's given us—after you've solved the case, of course."

"Of course," Giles said dryly. "Shall we make an appointment for Sunday night?"

"You mean you didn't invite him to the dinner, Sullivan?"

"He's not interested in crosswords, just cross words."

"I'll give him my ticket, Sullivan, so he can sit next to you."

"Nag, nag, nag, Macintosh. Oh, very well, I'll send Oliver over with a handwritten invitation. Satisfied?"

"Almost. Take me to Rumpelmayer's for a hot chocolate, then we'll go home. I came here for pleasure, remember? And I don't want to hear another word about murder until tomorrow morning. Got that, Sullivan?"

"Still trying to boss me around? Still nagging? God,

what will you be like after we're married?"

"That's one thing you'll never find out, Sullivan. But if you act lovable and mind your manners, you can get a lifetime simulation in Vermont."

 **20**

EVERYONE HAD COME EARLY. "SURE I'M NERVOUS," Lila said. "The first contest is tonight already, and we don't even know the dirt about one-third of the suspects."

"It's not just statistical," Caroline said. "The character of the person is more important. Some people just could not bring themselves to do certain kinds of things."

"You put pyrethrins on your violets, don't you?" Lila asked. "What's so different about putting cyanide into a rat?"

"There's a difference, Lila," Janos said. "Believe me, there's a big difference."

"Yeah, you can always get another violet," Vergil said, "if the bugs suck the life out of the one you have. But how would I get another life if a Harvey Brundage destroyed me?"

"Killing a human being is serious business," Norbert said, "which requires a lot of thought. It's not for joking."

"Who's joking?" Vergil asked. "If I were absolutely sure I'd get away with it, I wouldn't hesitate to kill half the people I write about, and I'd do it with less compunction than I'd kill an aphid. It would improve this old planet considerably."

"Whoever killed Harvey seems to be doing pretty good at getting away with it," Lila said.

"We're all pretty bright," Delmore said, "so that's to be expected. But Norbert's right; unless you've actually done it, you don't know. A sane person would have to be really driven to the wall to get to the point of killing a human being."

"Weren't we all driven?" Janos asked. "And I don't think any of us is crazy." He looked around for reassurance. "Crazy about crosswords doesn't count, of course."

"I think it was the *sane* thing to do," Lila said. "Who could figure the creep would strike back at us from the grave?"

"The killer evidently didn't," Giles said. "But it's too late to change things. What's done is done."

"Yeah," Lila said. "Instead of giving the exterminator a medal, we have to help find him for the cops. *That's* what's crazy."

Arthur Fredericks opened the conference room door and quietly placed the eight puzzles in front of Giles.

ACROSS

1 "Mighty ___ a Rose"
4 Throb
8 Musical conclusion
12 Possessive pronoun
13 Impel
14 New Zealand natives
16 Formal acceptance and
    effectuation
18 Pierce
19 Closing number
20 Venomous snake
21 Exclamation
22 Phase
23 The one here
25 1/4,840 of an acre: Abbr.
26 Metallic element
28 Water: French
29 Free ticket
32 Wife of Saturn
33 Enrages
36 Sick
37 John Jakes' *The* ___
39 Electric fish
40 A tempest in a ___
42 Him or her: French
43 Sole
44 Car workers' union: Abbr.
45 Break off
47 Shrewd
49 Card game
50 Accumulate
54 Grunting sound
55 Moo
56 Chess piece
57 Involve
59 Confirmed
61 Oozed
62 Silents star Jannings
63 Female ruff
64 Songbird
65 Companion to AMEX
66 Leatherworking tool

DOWN

1 Idles
2 Examine a tax form
3 Swedish coin
4 Manservant
5 A Great Lake
6 Earlier
7 X
8 Bivouac
9 "Alley ___"
10 Boring bee?
11 Choreographer Alvin
14 Fail to hit
15 Grain for sowing
17 Leaves
20 Intend
23 Upturns
24 Poolroom conman
25 Droop
27 Watercraft
28 Finish
29 Cherry stone
30 Beerlike beverage
31 Baseballer Enos
33 Operatic solo
34 Kinsman: Abbr.
35 Crafty
37 Violinist's need
38 Car
41 Salary
43 Of a unit of resistance
45 Crowlike bird
46 A wicked little thing?
47 Hints
48 Nixon's first veep
49 Crease
51 Greek marketplace
52 Xanthippe
53 Iron-based alloy
55 Mortgage interest
56 Singer Kristofferson
58 Imitate
59 Rooster's mate
60 Jimmy Carter's daughter

IMMORAL

21

"**I** CAN SEE BEFORE I FINISH," ISABEL SAID, "THAT FORTY-six Down is definitely you, Caroline."

"Just because I'm small?" Caroline said. "That's not fair."

"Don't be in such a hurry, Isabel," Lila said. "It can't be. The other puzzles had the dirt in the answers, not in the clues. And that clue is too good for the creep; I'm sure I saw it in a book recently."

"Did you get that thirty-seven Across?" Vergil asked. "I thought 'BRA' in the second puzzle was brave—some editors don't like the slightest sexual references—but this one . . . Wow!"

"The creep wasn't trying to sell his puzzles to an editor," Lila said. "He was shooting for bigger game. Us."

"Back at the old stand again, puzzle fans?" Isabel was really irritated. "You dopes would do puzzles on the way to the guillotine."

"Better than knitting," Lila said confidently, her pen flying across the paper, "Madame Defarge."

"We have a wealth of possible clues in this puzzle," Giles said quickly, before Isabel could flare up, "which in combination would cover half the criminal code of New York."

"Sure," Lila said, "but the first two puzzles had three words for each person, and creepy Harvey was a real square; he's bound to repeat himself. Let's work only on three-word combinations."

"In each of the first two puzzles," Janos said, "the Acrosses referred to one of us and the Downs to another. We should assume that the same applies here."

"Good idea," Lila said, capping her pen. "I'm done."

"So am I," Janos said a moment later. "Will you please get a lobotomy or something, Lila? You know what I need that first prize for."

"You want to see me go to jail, Janny? Tell you what: You don't enter the solvers contest and I won't enter the constructors contest. Save your strength and you'll have a better shot at winning that one."

"You call that a deal, Lila? You'll be lucky if you *finish* constructing by Wednesday. You're an idiot savant."

"Flattery will get you nowhere with me, Janny. Okay, folks, I have a set. 'BEAT,' 'IMPALE,' and 'ANGERS.' Self-explanatory."

"The theme," Caroline said, "is *Immoral*."

"By you impaling is moral, maybe? Not in my neighborhood."

"Along those lines," Vergil said, "there is 'KRIS,' 'SLAUGHTER,' and 'BUTLER.' A kris is a Malayan dagger. I've always wanted to be involved in a crime where the butler did it. How is Oliver with a knife, Giles?"

"Very good at roast beef," Giles said. "Now, stop kidding around and get down to business. This is Saturday, remember? The day before Sunday?"

"Here's a good one," Delmore said. "'AUDIT,' 'KRONA,' and 'PAY.' Someone is socking money away in Sweden. Or from Sweden. And will be exposed as soon as the books are checked."

"'DRAGQUEEN' must refer to you, Delmore," Isabel said. "It certainly can't mean Caroline, and you two are the only ones left."

"All sorts of straight men like to wear women's clothes, Isabel. You'd be surprised. Even their wives don't know, or their girlfriends." Delmore looked pointedly at Isabel. "And don't get your dander up. I'm not referring to anyone in particular. I'm just trying to show that this clue can't refer to me, that's all. I never wear women's clothes," he said stiffly. "If you like men, and your friend likes men, what's the point in trying to look like a woman?"

"'TIPS,' 'HUSTLER,' and 'BOAT,'" Vergil said. "Someone cheating at cards on ocean liners?"

"I have it," Caroline said. "'LAK,' 'CODA,' and 'OPS.' *Lak* is one hundred thousand rupees in India. *Coda* is a way of saying code, and *ops* is short for operatives. One of us is a spy." She tried very hard not to look at Giles. "And 'ASP' is a snake. And 'EEL,' as in 'slippery as an.' That makes a *five*-word set. All in Across."

"I see two other words in Across, Caroline," Isabel said, "that I would swear refer to you. The trouble is, I can't find the third word. Which one is it, Caroline?"

"None of your business," Caroline said defiantly.

"It is my business," Isabel said. "It's the business of all of us."

"I don't care," Caroline said stubbornly. "I'm not going to tell."

"You have to, Carrie," Lila said, "so Giles can find the murderer."

"But I didn't do it," Caroline insisted.

"Neither did I," Janos said, "and neither did anyone else. But one of us did."

"I can't help. *Nothing* I did had *anything* to do with Harvey's death."

"It's what he was blackmailing you about that counts," Vergil said. "It gave you a motive, same as the rest of us."

"I *admit* I had a motive. Can't you leave it at that?"

Isabel motioned the others to be quiet, then faced Caroline directly. "Listen to me, Caroline." Her voice had a schoolteacher's severe tone. "It's not enough to admit to a motive. We know that. It's the details, the character, the personality, that Giles must have, we all must have, so we can figure out who the killer is. It's Saturday morning already: the solvers contest is tonight. The constructors contest is tomorrow night. If as a result of your refusal to cooperate we don't solve the case by the time the prizes are presented, we're all lost. By next Wednesday everything you wanted to hide will be splashed across the country anyway. Is that what you want?"

"Maybe I'll win one of the prizes and go to Canada with Lila."

"That's nonsense," Isabel said firmly. "You can go to Canada right now. You're not an 'illegal' like Janos, or even an 'unethical' like Vergil. You're only an 'immoral.' Lila can't go because she needs a first prize to settle with the I.R.S., but what's keeping you?"

Caroline pressed her lips firmly together.

"Whatever you're trying to hide will come out even if you're in Canada, Caroline."

Caroline turned her head away.

"Very well, Trimble," Isabel said, "we will get to the bottom of this without you. And your stubbornness will be noted. Let's look at the puzzle. Here you are, Trimble. 'ADOPTION' and 'BASTARD.' Do you dare to deny it?"

"Don't you use that word." Caroline's face was twisted

in anger. "That's dirty—cruel. You're horrible."

"It's easy to see," Isabel said, "that you had a child out of wedlock, and that you gave it up for adoption. That isn't the only thing that's troubling you, I can tell, but let's build on that for a while. Consider that you haven't gone to Canada yet. Why? You've done nothing illegal or unethical. Librarians are so underpaid that you can get a job almost anywhere, so it isn't fear of starving in Canada that's holding you back. You don't have any important ties in New York that anyone knows about. The answer has to be that you want to, or need to, stay here. Why, Caroline?"

Caroline shot a quick look at Isabel, then snapped her eyes away. "The reasonable answer," Isabel said, "is that you didn't give the baby up blindly but that you had it adopted by a friend or relative. You wanted to keep the baby, even if you could not do so directly, so the foster parents must be within a day's round trip of New York City so that you could visit on special days: birthdays, Christmas, graduation. Presumably as an aunt, rather than as a mother, right? Don't try to hide your face, Caroline; I see I'm right."

"Leave me alone," Caroline cried. "I didn't do anything wrong. One mistake. I've paid for it. She's such a beautiful girl, with loving parents to take care of her. And she likes me."

"I don't doubt it," Isabel said soothingly. "And we don't really want to know her name or the names of her foster parents. It won't come out if we find the murderer, if you help us."

"Then stop now. I won't let you. . . . She'll be . . . Leave her alone. Please."

"So we've established," Isabel said, "that you had a child out of wedlock which you gave up for adoption to

114

a relative who lives near New York City. And you *don't* want to go through *that* experience again. You're not unattractive, but your hair is starting to go gray, yet you don't dye it, your clothes are, at best, serviceable, you avoid makeup, even lipstick. . . . Not exactly designed to attract men."

"My work and my daughter—I don't have time for anything else."

"Or money either, Caroline. Your second cousins, or whatever the relationship is, they sound like wonderful people, but they're not exactly rolling in money, are they, Caroline? When they adopted your little girl, you undertook to pay all additional costs, didn't you? Which leaves you a little short, doesn't it? That's not the latest designer fashion you're wearing, Caroline."

"I have enough. I do proofreading and copyediting; that's why I'm so busy."

Isabel turned to Rankin. "How much do free-lance proofreaders and copyeditors make, Delmore?"

"Enough to put a steak on the table and an occasional bottle of wine. An adjunct to the main income."

"Not enough to live on," Isabel concluded, "and not enough to support a young woman adequately. Especially at her age. She must be about ready to enter college, isn't she, Caroline?"

Caroline began crying softly into her handkerchief. Lila reached over and put her hand protectively on Caroline's shoulder. Isabel leaned forward, her face close to the weeping woman. "So we come to the third word," she said. "It's 'HARDCORE,' isn't it?"

"No," Caroline wailed. "No."

"Somehow," Isabel continued, "I don't see a forty-five-year-old woman making a fortune as a topless dancer, do you, Caroline? Or as an actress in X-rated movies?

No, Caroline, you're a word person. How many hundreds of rejection slips do you have at home? For the poetry, the plays, the serious novels, the historical love stories, the gothics, the juveniles, the sensuous romances? You couldn't sell any, could you? With all your skills, you were unable to produce commercial fiction. It's no sin, Caroline; most people in this world, no matter how talented, no matter how well taught, cannot write salable fiction.

"But there is one field that is relatively easy to break into; no agent required. One where, once you're in the publisher's stable of writers, everything you produce will be bought. It's a field where talent is less important than skill, where the ability to produce an exact number of pages is more important than sparkling dialogue, where attention to clinical detail is valued above characterization. A field where there is such an insatiable demand that if an author could produce a novel a month, it would be published almost automatically and, even more important, paid for as quickly."

Caroline, still crying, was turned completely into the back of her chair, knees drawn up. "Tell me, Delmore," Isabel said. "Could a writer produce one hardcore pornographic novel a month? How much could he earn this way?"

"Once you get into the swing of it," Delmore said, "I'm sure it's feasible. They're usually about half the length of a genre novel, and the first draft goes. The trouble is, it pays so little. After taxes and expenses, it could bring in only a few thousand a year."

"But added to whatever is earned by copyediting and proofreading, and whatever can be squeezed out of a librarian's salary, out of buying the cheapest clothes and the cheapest food, a loving mother could provide her beautiful daughter with the necessities of life, couldn't she, and occasionally a ribbon for her hair and maybe a chocolate malt?"

"I'm sure it could be done, Isabel," Delmore said. "But that's enough. You've found out what you wanted; now leave her alone."

"Can't," Isabel said. "I have more questions. Caroline, look at me. Are you a vegetarian?"

Caroline considered the question, then responded in a tearful whisper, "Not really. I eat seafood. Fish too. It's the higher orders..."

"Lots of nuts and seeds, Caroline?"

"You have to, to get a balanced diet."

"Do you eat the seed of hard-pit fruits? Peaches, plums, apricots, almonds?"

"Of course, but you have to—" She suddenly stopped.

"You have to put them in the oven first, right? At very high heat? For a long time? Why, Trimble?" Caroline turned her face to the chair back again and began crying softly. "Answer me, Trimble, or shall I do it for you?"

Isabel waited for a full minute. No response. "I'll tell you why, Trimble, although you obviously know. Because they're poisonous, Trimble, aren't they? You have to heat them, Trimble, to break down the poison, don't you? And do you know what the poison is, Trimble? Of course you do, or you wouldn't have stopped so suddenly. Cyanide, Trimble, good old cyanide."

"I don't know," came the muffled cry. "I don't know how to get the poison out."

"You're a librarian, Trimble; there's nothing you can't find out."

"That's enough, Isabel," Delmore said firmly. "Stop torturing her."

"One more word," Isabel said. "I really understand

your feelings, Caroline. I understand that you weren't concerned about our finding out your secret, but that you would do anything you could to prevent your daughter from being hurt. The trouble is, Caroline, if we don't find the killer, your daughter *will* be hurt. On Wednesday. And there's nothing you can do to stop it. Running away won't help; not cooperating won't help."

"Shut up," came the muffled cry from Caroline's chair. "Just shut up."

"When I'm finished," Isabel said. "If you don't win a first prize, tell your daughter to write to me, personally, at Windham University, in Rockfield, Vermont. It's a very good school; one of the best. If she has good grades— and I'm sure she has—I can arrange something: work, loans, scholarships that will let her complete her education." Isabel paused, then said, "Even if you're the murderer."

 **22**

"**A**M I GOING TO HAVE TROUBLE WITH YOU TOO?" Isabel asked.

"All I suggested," said Delmore mildly, "is that *you* don't question me. You're so shaken by what you did to poor Caroline that you're ready to *kill* me."

Isabel looked around at the others, saw what they saw. She took a deep breath and let it out slowly. Closing her eyes, she leaned back in her chair. "I'm sorry about Caroline," she said, "and I'm sorry you're all upset. But all this would have come out on Wednesday, *will* come out on Wednesday, if we don't find the killer. I did what I had to do, just as I would perform an appendectomy with a razor blade if there were no other way, or kill a suffering animal or be a midwife. We all have to do difficult things sometimes, even distasteful things. More harm or less harm, that's the choice." She opened her eyes. "I want to be friends with all of you or, failing that, at least not enemies. But if I have to—to save five of you, six, with Giles—I will do what I see my duty to do. I'd like to stay, but if you want me to leave now, speak up."

"I didn't say anything about leaving," Delmore said. "Just that you should observe. Silently."

"Thanks," Isabel said. "Will do. Wait. Norbert isn't here."

"It's Saturday," Janos said. "He'll be here after sundown. After supper, actually. I'll report to him about today's puzzle and about Caroline and Delmore. If he has any ideas, he'll discuss them with Giles before the contest starts."

"No one seems interested in my story," Delmore said. "Should I feel flattered or disappointed?"

"Both," Lila said. "So talk already. 'DRAGQUEEN' is you, isn't it?"

"I've never dressed in drag," Delmore said. "Harvey must have been at a loss for words to balance the construction. Sometimes"—he addressed Isabel—"sometimes, in constructing a puzzle, you use words you don't really want, words you are forced to use; otherwise you can't complete the puzzle. 'HUSTLER' doesn't really describe me either, not really, but I know what Harvey meant. And the best one"—he drew a deep breath—"the last one, is 'SLAUGHTER,' and that is completely inaccurate, completely. I'm made to look real bad because Harvey was a crummy constructor."

"I'm sure," Lila said kindly, "when you tell it, it'll come out better. Try, Delmore."

"I've never hidden that I'm gay," said Delmore, "even in high school. But heterosexuals have a peculiar ignorance about homosexuals. You think that we are promiscuous, that our lives revolve around homosexuality, that we have nothing on our minds but sex. Deny it if you will, but if you examine what your feelings are when you hear the word *faggot*, you'll see that even intelligent, educated people like you have these prejudices. The truth is that we do cluster together, we do spend a large part of our lives thinking about sex, and an even larger part of our lives is colored by homosexuality. But might that not be because of the attitudes and actions of the straight community?"

"If I," said Vergil, "or any of us, have caused you pain, Delmore, I apologize. It was unintentional and I—we—will do our best to see that it never happens again."

"You've been good friends," Delmore said, "and I love you all. I didn't mean... The point I wanted to make is that I want the same things you do: to love and be loved, to like and be liked, to work productively, to be respected, to make a living, to have a family—that sort of thing."

"You want children?" Lila asked.

"I don't think so, at least not right now. If I do—my sister doesn't want me hanging around her kids; the virus is catching, you know—I can adopt one. But not all families have children. There can be just the two of you."

"The fellow you're with now?" Vergil asked. "What's-his-name?"

"Yes, Charles. It's been three years. He's... We get along very well. I'd like—we'd both like it to be forever, till death do us part. It's important to me. To us."

"So who's stopping you?" Lila asked.

"If Brundage's poison comes out... Charles is very—conventional. It would kill him. He comes from a very rigid... His family is very stiff, unforgiving. They've finally accepted that he's gay, but they put him through hell first. They still haven't forgiven me for being of Italian descent."

"In this day and age?" Miklosz said. "You've changed your name?"

"Yes. After... I thought it would be better. My family doesn't want to... If my name gets into the papers, everyone will know they... So when I came to New York I called myself Delmore Rankin and had it changed legally a year later. But, of course, it's easy to trace."

"Tell us about the killing," Giles said.

"This man, my mentor actually, took me off the streets and into his home. He supervised and paid for my education, taught me about clothes, food, wine, art, theater, opened a whole new world to me. I respected him and I liked him."

"He was wealthy?" Lila asked. "You were his, uh, mistress?"

"Protégé was the word we used, but yes. He didn't pay—I had a little pocket money, but I never wanted for anything. He wasn't really wealthy, but he didn't have to work either. We were together for four years, and we could have been together still, if I hadn't . . ."

"Why did you kill him?" Janos asked. "It seems to me—"

"I didn't kill him. I told you, I liked him. Why should I kill him? It was—he was promiscuous; that was the problem. Just like some heteros."

"A prostitute?" Vergil asked. "A male prostitute killed him? Is that what the puzzle says? But how does that—"

"Everyone jumps to conclusions. If you wouldn't interrupt me . . ." Delmore drew a deep breath. "It wasn't that he didn't love me, but he had to have variety. One night he brought home a—rough trade, we call it—a violent man. Drunk. He was obviously the kind that preys on wealthy middle-aged gays. No sooner was he upstairs than he began beating my friend to get him to tell where the money was. I ran out of my room. My friend was on the floor at the top of the stairs. I ran at the monster—he was twice my size but I had to save . . . He swung at me. I slipped, the punch barely touched my face, and he lost his balance. He stepped on my friend and fell down the stairs. Broke his neck, thank God.

"I called an ambulance and the police. My friend's lawyer made a deal with the D.A. I took all the responsibility. I owed him so much, and my friend's name never got into the papers. I got three years' probation. Everybody was happy. I no longer owed my friend anything, but obviously, I could not live with him any longer either. Then I met Charles, and we've lived happily ever after."

"So you're afraid," Giles said, "that if Charles finds out you've been arrested for involuntary manslaughter, or whatever the charge was reduced to, he'd leave you?"

"Oh, no, I told him all about that. It's the—if he found out about it, he's...How would you feel, Giles, if you found out your wife had been a prostitute?"

"Were you really?"

"I was very young when I came here. I had no marketable skills, no friends, no place to live, no money, nothing. And I wasn't very street-smart either. Maybe it wasn't the best thing to do, but when you're hungry and alone and afraid...But *why* isn't important. The fact is, if Charles finds out..."

"If Charles really loves you, won't he forgive what happened in the past?" Vergil asked.

"Charles might; his family wouldn't. They'd cut him off in a second."

"Still," Vergil said, "two incomes..."

"Charles doesn't know how to work," Delmore said. "And I don't make enough."

"You have a very strong motive for killing Brundage," Giles said.

"Don't we all," Delmore said. "I also have a very strong motive for finding the murderer."

"Assuming *you're* not the killer," Isabel said.

"Wouldn't it be funny," Delmore said, "if this were

like an Agatha Christie story? The kind where the detective turns out to be the killer? Or the detective's friend? The one who is oh-so-busy trying to prove somebody else did it?"

 **23**

"I DON'T FEEL LIKE SITTING ON A PARK BENCH AGAIN, Giles."

"It was good enough for Bernard Baruch, Isabel, but whatever your heart desires. A hansom cab ride through the park?"

"I don't feel romantic now. Maybe after all this is over? Do you have any ideas on how to do it fast?"

"Nothing stands out. They all have strong enough motives. Character? Again, any one of them."

"Caroline and Delmore are not excluded now, are they?"

"Definitely not. Delmore especially. He's already killed once—you can't really believe his version of the story, even if the D.A. bought it—so why not again? And he really stood up to you, Isabel. That's something even I haven't been able to do."

"He happened to be right, Sullivan. If *you're* ever right, feel free."

"No thanks, Isabel, I'm not in the mood for sparring either. Where are you leading me?"

"Rumpelmayers. I need chocolate."

"How you keep your figure is beyond me. You must

put away a pound of chocolate a week."

"More. But only when I come to New York."

"New York? Or me?"

"Both. You're an irritant, Giles."

"I hope that's flattering."

"It could be, in the medical sense. You stimulate an inflammatory reaction."

"It's nice for a man my age to hear that he can still excite a beautiful woman."

"What I had in mind, Sullivan, was more like a pain in the ass. I came here to have a good time, a vacation. And what do I get? Sex and violence, in the wrong proportions. Hours of agony for moments of pleasure. I've had enough Wagner; comfort me with Schubert."

"Or chocolate? Here we are."

"And another thing, Sullivan: homburgs, chesterfields, and gold-headed canes went out with the Holy Roman Empire. I don't want to look like I'm being taken to the soda fountain by my grandfather."

"The hat and the coat are a disguise; ten seconds in a phone booth and *voilà*, Cary Grant."

"You may be better-looking, Sullivan, but he'd be more fun."

"I don't have fat little men with glasses writing my lines."

"At least the cane's gotta go, Sullivan. You're in better shape than most men half your age. Why a cane?"

"Protection. In Merrie Olde England the quarter staff was a deadly weapon. Besides, you don't need a license for a cane."

"There are no muggers in Vermont."

"There's not much of anything else, either. Remember, carnivores lead much more interesting lives than herbivores."

"I don't want an interesting life; I want—"

"I know exactly what you want. Miss, bring my grand-daughter here a super-duper hot chocolate with double everything."

"I changed my mind, Sullivan. Make that a chocolate soda with double everything. And a big side order of whipped cream with chocolate *and* vanilla syrup all over it and a cherry on top. Two cherries."

"I'll have a small order of vanilla ice cream."

"Vanilla, Sullivan? In public? Have you no shame?"

"He who loves the fair Macintosh, Macintosh, hath no need for more piquant stimuli."

"I sense that you're trying to make up for that unfor-givable blunder, Sullivan. The next sentence decides whether or not I give you one of my cherries to hide that shameful cold pale hemisphere."

"'Or might I of Jove's nectar sip/I would not change for thine."

"Did you make that up, Sullivan?"

"Of course, Macintosh, just for you. Four hundred years ago, when I was Ben Jonson and you naught but a tavern tart."

"Then I'm the first, Sullivan? You haven't tried it on anyone else?"

"The first and the only. I hereby swear and aver that this jewel of a line is a gift, freely given to Miss—Ms. Isabel Macintosh, as a token of the esteem in which I hold her, to have and to hold from this day forth, for-evermore."

"Oh, Giles, you really do love me. I've never gotten a better gift at a time I needed one worse."

"I do love you, Isabel, and to show there are no hard feelings, I will take a festive dollop of your whipped cream, with chocolate and vanilla syrup, to put on my ice cream."

"And to show that you are back in my good graces again, you may have..." She tore the top of the wrapping from her straw, blew into it hard, and hit him dead on the nose with the paper cylinder.

"I am sure," Giles said, "that the teenage delinquents you are surrounded by in your College of All-Too-Liberal Arts give off a deadly radiation that prevents the manifestation of maturity in a chronologically adult woman. Surely a granddaughter of your advanced years is capable of behaving in a more seemly manner in a respectable public establishment."

"The day you can't get any more stuffing into that shirt, Sullivan, is the day you're going to have to get a different dean to dally with, so watch yourself. Now, let there be worshipful silence while I fulfill my choco-erotic fantasies. I've gotten little enough pleasure in your company these past few days."

"Oh, my God!" Sullivan broke out. "Of course! *That's* how!"

"You're risking permanent banishment to the outer reaches, Sullivan. A gentleman does not interrupt a lady in the middle of—"

"It's all right, Isabel. I've got it. Look, you stay here. Finish your soda. I have to go home now, do some work. Go shopping. Here's some money. Go to Bloomingdale's. Buy anything you want. Come back in two hours. Make that three, that should be enough. Here's some more money. Have fun. 'Bye, darling."

🔸🔸🔸🔸🔸🔸🔸🔸🔸🔸🔸🔸🔸🔸🔸🔸🔸🔸 24 🔸🔸🔸

Isabel burst into Giles's study and dumped the packages on his desk. "I went shopping, darling," she said, "just as you ordered. Like a good little girl. And I got so many *wonderful* things. You'll be so proud of me, Grandpa, when you see what I got you."

"Isabel," he growled, "I'm busy. Can't this wait?"

"Don't you want to see what your empty-headed little fluff bought for all the nice money you gave her? Look at this: a training bra, so when your next little girlfriend grows up, you'll have it all ready."

"Isabel—"

"And here. Cherry lollipops. For positive reinforcement. When she does something *exactly* right. And a box of gold stars, so she can have a permanent record to show her mommy."

"Macintosh, I'm warning you—"

"A book: *What Every Young Girl Should Know*. Saves you teaching her the missionary position. It has diagrams. And a whip, to help her learn faster; a little negative reinforcement goes a long way with mules and women."

"I don't know what's gotten into you, Macintosh, but—"

"And the prize: a genuine antique, from 1894, a primer of etiquette, Victorian. She can learn how to curtsy, to sit with her knees together, and to speak when spoken to."

"Is that all, Macintosh?"

"I could have done much better, Sullivan, if I thought you were worth the time. Where the hell do you get off treating me like a—a wife? I don't have to take this crap. I'm a big girl now, in case you hadn't noticed. You want a dizzy teenage robot you can shove a pacifier into her mouth, a shopping spree or a beauty parlor, you can have her, but that's not me. You said you loved me, you lying son of a bitch. Is this how you treat people you love? What the hell was so important that— What are you working on, crosswords? My God, Sullivan, you've really done it this time. You walked out on me to do a CROSS-WORD?"

"I can explain, if you'll only listen."

"Listen? You want me to listen? Okay, I'll listen. I want to see how you get out of this one. Start lying."

"It's all very simple. I had to, that is, I wanted—it was really necessary to . . . It was to solve the case."

"A brilliant exposition, Sullivan. Why didn't I think of that? And now that it's been fully explained to me, now that I understand, am I obliged to forgive? Sullivan, in some colleges they give courses in remedial reading and remedial writing for those students who were favored with progressive education. You were exposed to law school for several years; didn't they have courses in remedial lying?"

"Oliver!" Sullivan shouted.

"No need to shout, sir. I was listening at the door."

"Why did you let her in?"

"She was very determined, sir. The Scots, you know."

"You let a civilian, a woman, get past you?"

"I did not wish to inflict bodily harm, sir. Miss Macintosh is a favored guest of the staff. And I thought perhaps it was time that she became aware . . . I did, however, ascertain that she was not carrying a deadly weapon anywhere on her person."

Isabel stiffened. "You did what, Oliver?"

Oliver moved back calmly. "Very discreetly, Miss Macintosh, I assure you. No offense was intended."

"Wait a minute," Isabel said, sitting down. "Something funny is going on here. What's that puzzle you're working on, Sullivan?"

Giles slid the papers together on his desk. "Just a puzzle, darling. To relax."

"I don't need to see it, Sullivan; it's all clear to me now. You're Hannibal, the infamous, anonymous crosswords expert."

"Why, what a silly—"

"Don't insult my intelligence, Sullivan. It all fits. Everything Delmore told me about Hannibal. The secrecy, the coincidence of your wife's death eighteen years ago and Hannibal's first construction. Having the checks sent directly to a charity. Breaking the rules to show off a super pun. And above all, telling me I mustn't enter the contest—it all fits. And you never told me, Sullivan? That's the way to start a marriage? With secrets?"

"But we're not married."

"That doesn't matter. If we were married, would you have told me? No! And your absences? You would have let me think you were with another woman when you were really ditching me to construct a crossword. That's low, Sullivan. Really low. And how come you're always so busy, Sullivan? You retired three years ago. What the hell are you doing? It sure as hell isn't only crosswords."

"The Cruciverbal Club takes a lot of my time. Then there are my many charitable—"

"You're the worst liar for a lawyer I've ever seen; however did you pass your bar exam? It might have been real easy in the olden days. Why don't you tell me the truth for a change, Sullivan? I could take your being an international jewel thief; I might even enjoy helping... Wait! Barker! That call from Barker the other day. Who is Barker?"

"An old friend, darling. Just wanted to see how I was."

"Bullshit, Sullivan! It isn't Bark*er*; it's Barc*a*. Hamilcar Barca, Carthaginian general, around 250 B.C. Father of Hannibal. He's your control, or whatever they call it, isn't he? You're a spy, Sullivan. A goddamn spy!"

"You're really upset, Isabel. I'm sorry. Would you like a drink?"

Isabel leaned forward in her chair and pinned him with her eyes. "Stop it, Giles. It's too late. So Barca heard you were sick? Ha! You haven't been sick a day in your life. And Oliver told him it was a slight cold? That you would soon be better? What's that code for? Are you in trouble, spy? Slight, but it will be over soon? A code for calling at home over an unsafe phone? And his asking if you needed antibiotics? To kill germs? Or to kill the people who are making trouble for you? Call him if you need anything? Anything? Bribe a politician? Pressure the police? Wipe out Albania? Talk, Sullivan, and this time it'd better be good. Real good."

Giles looked at her steadily. She was on the verge of tears. "Isabel," he said, "I am not quite a spy. During the war I worked with Signal Intelligence, heading a cryptanalysis section. At times I worked with people in O.S.S. and British Intelligence. After the war I was occasionally called in to do specific bits of work, all involving codes. Barca is the person who contacts me. Naturally, he was concerned that I was involved in a murder case; an investigation might have revealed my governmental connections. The newspapers would have distorted everything. The headlines would have read: INTERNATIONAL FINANCIER POISONED IN CIA HOUSE. So Barca called to see if his help was needed in killing—squelching—adverse publicity."

"Do you work for the C.I.A., Giles? Is that why Lieutenant Faber didn't question us again? Is that why you're so eager to solve this case? Are you worried that next Wednesday's papers will expose you as a spy?"

"I work *with*, not *for*, a small specialized organization which does not, I think, have a connection with the C.I.A., although it is possible that the C.I.A. may call on it occasionally for expert advice. I think it highly probable that Lieutenant Faber was told that I and you, naturally, were not to be considered suspects. I am eager to solve this case because I want the law upheld, and I want my friends to suffer no more pain, but I am also deeply concerned that I and my connections do not appear in the newspapers."

"Oliver is part of your spy ring, isn't he?"

"Oliver knows everything I know, but his main function is to take care of me and this house."

"Take care? You mean protect? Oliver?"

"Don't be misled by his age, Isabel, or his size and shape. Oliver could take me apart in ten seconds. He was trained by Fairbairn."

"Ping too? He's the karate expert, right?"

"Ping is a linguist—Asiatic languages. Of course, he is skilled in the use of some weapons, as we all are."

"This is crazy," Isabel said, standing up. "I'm getting out of here." When she turned, Oliver was standing in front of the door, relaxed, hands at his sides.

"Please sit down, Isabel. I assure you that I am not a spy. I analyze codes, nothing more, and I do it for love. Love of law, love of country, love of peace, love of everything you yourself think of as good. My work has helped some people directly; that I know. Those it has hurt, and there have been some, were the ones who were hurting innocent people, terrorizing people, killing people. You've known me intimately for over fifteen years; could you have loved an evil man?"

"I'm not sure; you fooled me successfully for those fifteen years. How do I know you're not fooling me now? I didn't realize how much smarter you are than I am. And you're keeping me prisoner here."

"I'm not smarter than you, Isabel, just smart in a different way. Which is as it should be."

"Sir," Oliver reminded him, "you are evading the issue."

"So I am, Oliver, so I am." Giles came from behind his desk and kneeled at the side of Isabel's chair. He took her limp hand in his and spoke solemnly. "Isabel Macintosh, I have loved you from the minute I met you. I want to be with you, to share my life with you, to devote my life to making you happy. Will you do me the honor of becoming my beloved wife?"

She looked at him dully. "Why now? Why in front of Oliver? Is this so I won't talk? What happens if I refuse?"

"I've proposed to you before, Isabel, many times, when you knew nothing about my work. I proposed because I love you. I meant it then; I mean it now."

"I refused you then; do you think I would accept you

under these conditions? What are you going to do, kill me?"

Giles turned pale. "I couldn't bring myself to hurt you in any way, Isabel." He stood up.

"That unpleasant duty, Miss Macintosh," Oliver said, "would become my responsibility. I beg you to reconsider."

"No. This is not the way to marry."

"Very well," Giles said, "then we'll run away together. Oliver, for old times' sake . . . I will accept full responsibility for Miss Macintosh."

"Why don't you just retire, Giles?"

"There is no retirement possible for me, Isabel. I, uh, am too deeply involved. It would be dangerous if I were no longer part of the organization."

"Dangerous for you, Giles, or dangerous to the organization?"

"Both. But Oliver, you know that I would do nothing that could in any way—"

"I'm afraid, sir, you are not thinking very clearly. Is there not a better alternative?"

"You would give up everything, Giles?" Isabel asked. "Risk everything? Run away with me? Live in South America? Africa?"

"Whither thou goest, Isabel, there go I."

"What's *your* alternative, Oliver?" Isabel asked. "Join the club?"

"Precisely, Miss Macintosh." Oliver smiled. "That you saw the solution so quickly adds to your qualifications. Your recent interest in crosswords—" He raised his hand to stop her words. "Oh, yes, Barca has been considering the possibility that you might join us for some years now; it is surprising that Mr. Giles has been able to keep his activities secret from such a clever woman for so long."

"I belong to some very subversive organizations," she said.

"Petitions for Mr. McGovern and the Committee for a Free Press are not what we would consider a danger to the American way of life. You do understand that you would enter at the very lowest level, but only until your ability is proven."

"Does that mean I'll have to take orders from Sullivan?"

"Only professionally, Miss Macintosh."

"I'll think about it," Isabel said. "In the meantime, Sullivan, I asked a question that you've been evading. What's that puzzle you're working on?"

Giles went to the chair behind his desk. "I'm constructing a new puzzle for the solvers contest. I have to have it ready for tonight, copied and packaged. Oliver, find Mr. Winston, tell him *not* to deliver the bundle of puzzles to the club tonight, nor the other bundle tomorrow night. I want the copying machine, the big one, turned on, so it's hot when I get there. Have him instruct the building security people that I'll—we'll be there at five or six. You'll have to help me, Isabel."

"What good will a new puzzle do?" Isabel asked. "The only words in it will be yours."

"It will make the killer nervous. I'll put words in it that only the killer will recognize. The killer will be sure I know who he is and say something, do something, that will cinch it."

"You know who it is? Tell me."

"I think I know, but there's no way to prove it. You can't accuse a person of murder on guesswork."

"You think the killer will try to kill you, Giles? You're offering yourself as bait?"

"Possibly, but I doubt anything overt will happen to-night. It's just a pressure tactic. What I'd like you to do, Isabel, is—you won't enter the contest, will you?—good. What I'd like you to do is get a copy of the six solutions, the ones by the six directors, and bring them to me as soon as they're turned in. There may be some indications —erasures, uneven pressures on the pencil—things like that."

"It sounds like you're grasping at straws, Giles."

"I'm almost positive, Isabel, it couldn't have been done any other way. If I hadn't been trained as a lawyer, I would say I'm sure. But *tomorrow's* contest, that will do the trick. I hope. I have something in mind for that one."

"If there is a possibility of danger, sir, perhaps I should be present," Oliver said. "Perhaps as a waiter?"

"That's a good idea, Oliver. Isabel, would you call Lila and arrange it? And now I'll go back to work. Close the door behind you, Isabel. I have to ask Barca for something and you haven't signed up yet."

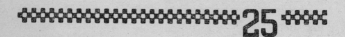 **25**

"**A**LL SIX ARE SEATED IN ONE SECTION," ISABEL SAID. "The copying machine is in the judges' room, so it'll be easy for me to make an extra set. Caroline was overjoyed when I offered to run the copier."

"Good," said Giles. "I'll be making the announcement soon. Give our copies extra contrast, so any little deviation will stand out. Who's taking care of the originals?"

"They go through a slot in a sealed box, in case anyone challenges the judges' decision, though I don't see what's to challenge in this contest."

"When every second counts, it's possible to make one letter that looks like another." Giles looked at his watch. "Time to go."

Suddenly Giles stopped. "Isn't that a new dress you're wearing?"

"So you finally noticed, Sullivan? Cary Grant would have said, 'You look especially lovely tonight, my dear. On you that gown is absolutely fetching.' *Gown*, Sullivan, is what it's called by the urbane lover, not *dress*."

"What I meant was, where, that is, when—"

"You ordered me to go shopping, didn't you? And you showered me with gold, right? So I went shopping."

"But I thought you were angry."

"I knew you'd worm your way back into my good graces. I just wanted to see how you'd do it. Quit while you're ahead, Sullivan; it's a lot easier to worm your way out of favor than to get back in, and you're moving very fast for a man with one foot in his mouth. So shut up and announce while I polish my makeup. I hear Cary Grant's in the audience tonight; I want to make his trip worthwhile."

All the sliding doors and folding panels had been pushed aside, turning the first floor of the old Cornelius van Broek mansion into the ballroom his wife had insisted on. Every square foot of the white oak parquetry was covered with student desks packed so closely there was scarcely room to squeeze between them. If anyone is stupid enough to cheat, Giles thought, he won't be able to finish in time to get near the top fifty. With speed demons like Lila, Janos, and Norbert competing, anyone who so much as raised his eyes from the contest puzzle automatically dropped ten places.

There was a soft hum in the huge room, conversation politely kept low so as not to annoy a neighbor but multiplied by hundreds of voices. An air of expectancy—tense, nervous, Giles could sense it—of people waiting for the starting shot, waiting to jump ahead, to take the lead, to win. Not just the money, although to most it was crucial and, to six, at least, a matter of life and death, but for the distinction, the honor, the glory of being best.

The microphone had been placed at the end of the corridor, exactly at the entrance to the ballroom. Giles tapped the mike with his pencil. The room became silent at once, the silence even more edgy than the prior hum.

"I had intended," Giles said, "to make a long, boring

speech to relax you"—there was a titter of nervous laughter—"but I would be most distressed if anyone did not wake up in time to—" The laughter stepped on the rest of his words. "So," Giles continued, "a quick review of the rules. The contest puzzles are being distributed, placed on your desk facedown. If you touch your puzzle before the signal, you are disqualified.

"When I give the signal, turn your sheet over and work as quickly as you can. Ink is preferred, but a dark, sharp pencil is acceptable. Block letters only. If your answers are not perfectly legible, you're disqualified.

"This is a test of speed, but your solution must be perfect. Considering the caliber of the people here tonight—I see many old friends—a single mistake will put you very far down on the list. But don't let that discourage you; some of our past winners were in the bottom ten percent their first times out.

"As soon as you are finished, take your solution to the nearest time stamper. That's where the red pennants are flying. If you require, a messenger will pick up your entry; just raise your hand. Don't raise it when you're done; raise it ten seconds before, so the messenger can snatch the solution off your desk the moment you form the last letter.

"A word of advice: Don't worry about how fast the others are working or how many you see going to the time stampers. Just do your level best, your personal best; no one can ask more of you. In all cases, whether it's who gets to the clock first or whose writing is illegible, the decision of the judges is final. Your judges are well-known professionals who will be introduced and will receive plaques of appreciation after the dinner tomorrow, just before the prizes are awarded. One last bit of good news:

The contest puzzle was constructed by Hannibal"—a wave of groans swept the room—"but all the conventions were observed. The theme, which was deliberately left off the puzzle sheet to foil those of you with X-ray vision, is *Missiles*. Get ready, get set, GO!"

26

ISABEL JOINED GILES ON THE PODIUM. EVERY HEAD IN the big ballroom was down, working furiously. The runners stood like sheepdogs, eyes darting here and there, trying to watch in all directions at once.

"Come back into the office, Giles," Isabel said. "I'd like to go over tomorrow's plans."

"I can't leave now, Isabel, and neither can you. You'd better get over to the copying machine now."

"Are you kidding, Giles? The contest just started."

"How long do you think it takes a champion to print sixty-five words? These people are *good*. You saw how quickly they did the puzzles Brundage sent."

ACROSS

1 & 17 Ad exhortation
    4 It's set in a setting
    7 Pushers' foes
   12 Felt intensely
   18 Time of your life
   19 "If __ Would Leave You"
   20 John Peter Wagner
   21 Place to use a pencil
   23 Expunged
   24 Pinch pennies
   25 Asparagus servings
   26 Win __ nose
   27 Spidey's logo
   29 Iso-
   30 Everyone in Italy
   31 Mashie or niblick
   32 Quite brief condensation
   34 Writer's archenemy?
   36 Superfluous
   38 Timetable abbr.

39 Telephoned: Abbr.
42 Incomplete eight?
43 Cabbage kin
46 Mao's successor
47 Broadway fiasco
49 Heat units: Abbr.
50 Markedly abrupt
54 Part of the foot?
56 Hardly the bigshots!
58 Penultimate star?
59 Moon of Jupiter
61 Moves suddenly
62 Spangle
63 Boom time
64 Medicinal pills, e.g.
66 Cross and Kupcinet
67 ___ Domingo
68 Villain of the 1940s
69 Garden intruder
71 Pot-pie veggie
72 Rival
75 Dander
76 Draft initials
77 Khan, for one
80 Windborne loam
   deposit

81 Pedestrians with
   packs
84 Wes Unseld's team
86 Double agent who
   plans ahead
87 Sample
91 Agree
92 H.S. subj.
94 Arctic bird
95 Signpost signs
96 Story of Paris?
98 Forward
100 Ultraconventional
   types
101 "Shut up!"
102 Down Under city
103 Pie filling?
104 Ewe said it
105 "___ Remember"
106 Collegian's furlough
107 Polygraph's
   discernment
108 The limit, maybe

DOWN

1 "___ of robins..."
2 Nutria
3 Canaryish comment
4 Any of three in a
Sherlock Holmes adventure
5 "I" strains?
6 Catcall?
7 Apple with appeal?
8 Bird-related
9 D.C. V.I.P.
10 Cox's charges
11 Brandy cocktails
12 Oohs' mates
13 Soda-shoppe orders
14 Matchless
15 Commotion
16 Saw

22 Restrain
26 Streetwise pal
28 *A Fool There Was* star
31 1973 song, "Hello ___"
33 Little rock
35 Weather-map line
36 Jewish village
37 Assets
39 First Super Bowl losers
40 Small crescent shape
41 Polyester fiber
44 Ohio campus
45 Basra local
48 Nurses' burdens, at
times
51 Commandeers
52 Pares

53 *Wizard of Oz* locale
55 Instruction book
57 Folksinger Joan and kin
58 Guarantee
60 Streisand hit
65 Perpendicular, so to speak
68 Hopeless situation
70 "Frailty, thy name is..." this woman
73 Kitchenware
74 Opinion
77 Servile
78 Elvis's prop

79 Erie Canal terminus
82 Sort
83 Teasdale
85 On the level
86 Largest of the rays
88 Rowan trees
89 Nose job?
90 Type of exam question
93 Holly
95 "___ *se habla español*"
97 DDE's WWII command
99 Prospector's desire
100 Size selection: Abbr.

SOLVERS CONTEST

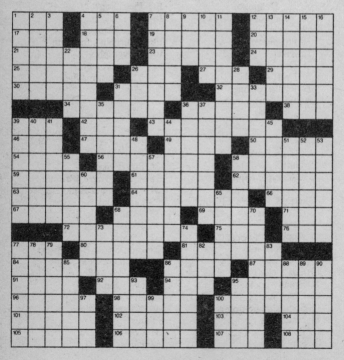

144

"But those were little ones, fifteen by fifteen. This one is bigger and harder, isn't it?"

"It's a little bigger and a little harder, that's all. I'll bet there are twenty people who'll come in under ten minutes."

"Under ten minutes? For a nineteen by nineteen? I don't believe it."

"Figure it out for yourself. A nineteen by nineteen has three hundred sixty-one squares. The usual conventional puzzle has between fifteen and seventeen percent black squares, which leaves about three hundred boxes to fill in. At a second a box, that's five minutes."

"But they have to read the clues. And think. And if they don't know something, they have to check the words that cross it."

"Lila's not the only one who uses the Across-only technique. You put your left forefinger on the Across column and move it slowly downward, clue by clue, while your right hand fills in the boxes."

"And if you're stuck?"

"That rarely happens. But if you are, you just keep going. A few more words filled in on the next lines and you can get the words you missed by doing an occasional Down."

"What about mistakes, Giles? I heard what you said about one mistake disqualifying you."

"These people don't make mistakes; they're the best. Do you think they'd work in ink if they thought they could make a mistake?"

"That's just showing off, Giles."

"No, it isn't. A razor-point pen makes a very neat letter. You don't have to worry about the point of your pencil breaking, or not making a clean line if it's too dull. You don't have the fear of tearing the paper if your point is too sharp. Would you believe that some of them, Lila for one, make very small letters because it saves fractions of a second per letter?"

"Boy, am I glad I withdrew; I'd have come in a bad last."

"This year, Isabel, yes. Next year? I'm not so sure. I have a feeling you'd be in the top fifty percent."

"Look, Giles! Lila!" Lila was holding her left hand high in the air and writing furiously with her right. Just as she lifted her pen, a runner picked up her puzzle and squeezed his way to a time clock.

Twenty seconds later, Janos Miklosz lifted his hand. A minute after that, three more hands were in the air. Then Caroline Trimble, along with six others. Norbert Kantor now, and there were hands all over. Some people were moving to the timeclocks themselves. Delmore Rankin was next and, a full minute later, Vergil Yount raised his hand.

"You'd better get over to the judges' room, quick," Giles said. "Get copies of the six directors' puzzles and meet me in the conference room as soon as you can get away."

27

"I DON'T SEE ANYTHING IN THESE PUZZLES," ISABEL said. "Do you?"

"Nothing. They're all so neatly filled out, they could almost have been typed."

"Who would have thought that Caroline would come in before Norbert?"

"I would have," Giles said. "Wait until you know her better. Just because she's shy doesn't mean her brain is slow. And she has an almost photographic memory."

"Do you think Lila will win the constructors contest too?"

"Not a chance; her mind doesn't work that way. My money is on Norbert, with Janos giving him a good fight. Vergil will come in within the first ten, and Delmore won't be too far behind him. Caroline will be in the first twenty. Lila will be way back, but surely in the top fifty."

"You know, Giles, if Janos comes in second in the constructors contest, too, he'll have a total of twenty thousand, almost enough to get his mother out."

"He's a good businessman. I'm sure he'll figure out a way. If not, maybe I'll find a way to lend him and the others money in a way that won't embarrass them."

"Even the killer?"

"The people they were trying to help should not suffer just because . . . Harvey Brundage was . . . In real life, things are not always clear-cut, black or white, good guys against bad guys."

"You don't have to lend anyone anything, Giles; just find the killer. Then Vergil will have time to replace the money, Delmore won't lose his lover, I can help Caroline's daughter, Norbert won't have to run to Israel, and Janos will surely have enough money for his mother. Lila's all set, if only she knew it."

"She knows it, Isabel; she could see she was first."

"She still has to worry that she made a mistake without noticing it. I know she didn't take the time to check her Downs. I wish I could tell her."

"Don't even think of it. One of these six killed Harvey Brundage. Until we're sure we know who it is, we have to keep the pressure on all of them."

"I thought you knew who did it."

"I think I do, but I'm not sure. As a lawyer, I feel it must be beyond a reasonable doubt. We'll have to wait for tomorrow's contest."

"You've set a trap?"

"Sort of. Actually, what I'm doing is letting the killer trap himself. I've set up the construction and the theme, and a few other gimmicks, so as to allow or, rather, encourage the killer to identify himself."

"Why should he, Giles? If I were the killer, I would construct the puzzle so carefully that I would avoid any reference at all to anything that could tie me to the murder."

"That would be highly suspicious in itself. Besides, that's the one thing the killer cannot do. The nonkillers are hoping for, counting on, the killer's being caught before Wednesday. The killer must count on his *not* being caught. Therefore he has to get away before Wednesday to avoid whatever he killed Harvey for. He *must* win a prize, preferably first prize. And the only way he can do it, given the quality of the people he's competing against, is to work as well and as fast as he can. If he does that, whatever is burning in his mind must surface. What I did tonight will pressure him even more; it will be in the forefront of his mind when his guard is down, when he's concentrating on a puzzle, trying for speed."

"I get it. It's like a psychological word-association test."

"Worse. There can be no retraction, no smoothing over. The puzzle I constructed, or rather the blank I set up, is not an easy one. Lots of big white blocks requiring relatively long words and difficult crossings. And the theme ... There is no way he can hide from me. Once he puts down a word, even if he finds it leads him where he doesn't want to go, there is no way he can change it in time. With all the crossings he'd have to change, he might as well quit right then and there. What he puts down must stay. His only hope is that I really know less than I think I know."

"Won't he try to change the clues, to make the words he had to put down appear to have meant something else? Something less harmful to him?"

"He can, but how will that help? You're supposed to put down clues that are accurate but misleading; that's half the fun, and the constructor is given extra credit for doing just that. In fact, the wit and cleverness of the clues will play a very important part in the judges' decisions. While the constructor is trying to think up wild and funny clues at top speed, his censor will be pushed into the background. Whatever is on his mind will come out. It's like being warned, when you're about to meet someone important, not to mention his large nose. You think so much about it that you greet him with, 'I'm very pleased to meet you, Mr. Nose.' Hasn't that ever happened to you?"

"Just last year at the school," Isabel said, "we were giving an honorary degree to Mr. Bailey, who was very sensitive about his weight. I introduced him as Mr. Belly." She smiled ruefully. "It got a big laugh."

"Exactly," Giles said. "It doesn't matter how brilliant the killer is; at the speed with which he'll be working, he's got to slip. It's a technique some psychiatrists use. At the first meeting the patient can talk about anything, start anywhere; it doesn't matter. In a surprisingly short time, whatever is troubling the patient will be expressed, either directly or indirectly. Lawyers use the same technique with reluctant clients and witnesses."

"The killer has another hope, Giles: that even if you know for sure who he is, you can't prove it in court. He still goes free, collects the money, and his secret is safe. Unless..."

"Unless what, Isabel?"

"Unless you do what he is most frightened of, what he killed Harvey Brundage for—threaten to expose what you learned from Harvey's puzzles, to expose his crimes to the world right then and there at the dinner, in front of all the reporters, so he doesn't have time to get away to Canada."

"I couldn't do that." Giles was shocked. "That information was given in confidence."

"You weren't retained as his attorney, Giles."

"It would be dishonorable."

"What about your duty, Giles? Aren't you an officer of the court? Sworn to uphold the law? A murder was committed, Giles. What do you do about it?" Giles looked tortured. "Of course," Isabel said, "Harvey Brundage was a rat of the first water. He deserved to die, didn't he? His murderer should get a medal, right, Giles?"

"Why are you doing this to me, Isabel?"

"Me? I'm not doing anything; you're doing it to yourself. I have a suggestion. Percival will be at the dinner tomorrow night. Ask him what he'd do."

"No. I have to decide. When the time comes, I'll do what is right. By my own standards. Not Percival's, not yours, not anyone else's. Mine."

"Good. I was just testing to see if you were sufficiently human to have the continued privilege of sharing my bed. I'm glad you're sweating. A glib answer and you would have slept alone tonight, much to my frustration. And Giles, maybe I *will* join your little gang of nonspies. Any group that would stand for an introspective, indecisive Hamlet type like you can't be all bad. Or all that competent. Start me at the bottom, will they? Give me a year and I'll be running the whole shebang myself."

28

"OLIVER, ARE YOU CARRYING A GUN?"

"Certainly not, sir. All my guns are too big to hide in a waiter's jacket."

"You have that confident look, Oliver. Safe and secure."

"When one is on the side of the angels, sir, and the heart is pure..."

"So you *are* carrying something. A cosh?"

"A little sand in a flexible sack, sir. Not enough to make a bulge."

"And a knife perhaps?"

"I do happen to have a sharp instrument, sir. At a formal dinner a waiter is sometimes called on to—"

"Only one knife?"

"Only one with a handle, sir."

"How many throwing knives?"

"Only two, sir. I have put on a bit of weight, sir, and the uniform is too tight to—"

"No other weapons?"

Oliver looked hurt. "In deference to your wishes, sir, I am practically defenseless."

"That's a rather large ring, Oliver."

"An heirloom, sir. My sainted aunt."

"The other one is even larger, Oliver."

"I come from a large family, sir."

"Is that an oversized belt buckle I see outlined on your cummerbund?"

"Help the posture, sir. I do have a bit of a tummy."

"Seems extraordinarily narrow for a support belt, Oliver. Your shoes look rather heavy too."

"Arch supports, sir. Serving does take its toll."

"So we are all set, are we, Oliver?"

"As well as can be expected, sir, under your restrictions."

"You will also remember to ignore me and to keep an eye on Miss Macintosh no matter what happens?"

"I was always very fond of the lady, sir, and now that she has decided to cast her lot with ours, what was once my pleasure is now my duty. But won't it look odd, sir, for you to carry a large can into a formal dinner?"

"It would look even odder, Oliver, if the cloakroom attendant accidently twisted the shaft."

"Your point is well taken, sir. You may be interested to hear that I have arranged with the other waiters that I will serve the six directors as well as you and Miss Macintosh."

"I don't expect that sort of trouble, Oliver, but it was a sensible precaution. How much?"

"Two hundred, sir. Waiters are so avaricious these days. In the old days at the Savoy a shilling would have sufficed."

"Money well spent, Oliver. As the Bible says, 'Muzzle not the ox that treadeth out the corn.' I see it is almost time to announce the big contest. Will you find Miss Macintosh, please, and ask her to take her seat, since I will be unable to escort her. You will find her in the bar, no doubt, with a cocktail in each hand, surrounded by a large group of short fat men with glasses who are regaling her with the lines they wrote for Cary Grant."

"It's her new gown, sir. Very fetching indeed."

29

THIS EVENT WAS NOT AS NOISY AS THE SOLVERS CON-
test. The desks were farther apart and the contestants
more serious. They appeared at ease, relaxed, and confident. It fooled no one. The lightest touch would have
sent any one of them twanging through the ceiling. Each
had a box of fine-line push-type mechanical pencils on
his desk. No ink this time; construction wears down eras-
ers faster than it does lead.

Giles and Isabel surveyed the contestants. "A motley
crew," she said. "If you met any of them on the subway,
you'd clutch your bag closely and keep your back to the
door."

"They happen to be among the most clever and quick-
witted people in New York," Giles said. "You can't tell
by appearances, you know. And isn't that *another* new
dress, uh, gown?"

"Spoken like a true clod, Sullivan, a veritable slow-
witted oaf. But be of good cheer, Sullivan; you're im-
proving. This time it took you only an hour to notice that
I look *heavenly* tonight."

"But—but—another?"

"An elegant lady would not be seen dead in the same

155

gown in the same place on two consecutive evenings, even though it looked particularly *heavenly* on her, would she?"

"You bought *two*?"

"You thrust money on me twice, Sullivan, remember? Whatever made you think I would spend *all* my hard-gotten gains on gifts for you alone? Don't I deserve a crumb off the table?"

"You deserve a spanking, Macintosh, that's what."

"Oh, Giles," she cooed, "you've been reading the manuals again. How sweet."

"I'll talk to you later," he said. "It's time to start the contest."

"Your face is all red, dear," she said. "Take a deep breath from your diaphragm and repeat after me: 'Om mani padme hum.' There now, don't you feel *much* better?"

"**L**ADIES AND GENTLEMEN," GILES SAID INTO THE MI-
crophone, "the constructors contest is about to begin.
There have been a few changes in the rules, so please
listen carefully." The room was totally quiet.

"A contest of this kind must, by its very nature, be
judged subjectively. It is easy to record the time of com-
pletion, and speed is a very important factor, but that is
hardly enough. Any skilled constructor can build a crossword puzzle following all the conventions and using only
legal words in a relatively short time. He can provide
simple, accurate clues in an even shorter time. But is this
what we really want?

"Does not a large part of our pleasure come from puzzles that have difficult and unusual arrangements of words,
that solve crossing problems with a minimum of the cliché
short words? Don't we all love the clever, the witty, the
humorous, the unusual clue? Isn't it exciting to see how
many theme words can be effectively fitted into a puzzle?
And shouldn't we, therefore, give extra consideration to,
additional credit for, these elements of delight? Of course
we should, and when we judge a puzzle, we do. But this
judgment is highly subjective, and in the past we have

heard rumblings of disagreement with the decisions rendered by our august judges."

"Anytime I don't win," shouted a voice from the audience, "it's a fix."

"My sentiments precisely," Giles agreed. "So this evening we are making an attempt to increase the objective measurements. Speed, of course, will still be the most important factor. But we will also give points for the number of theme words used; that is, the more words used in the puzzle that are directly related to the theme, the more points given. The average length of the theme words used will also be considered. That is, the greater the total number of letters in the theme words, the more points. For example, if the theme is *Rodents*, 'CAPYBARA' will give more points than 'RAT.' Is that clear?" There was a murmur of agreement.

"Then we will give points for unusual theme words, words that are rarely used in crossword puzzles. This will be, to some extent, subjective, but if all three judges agree that a word is special, that puzzle will gain points. Obscenities, I regret to say, are so common these days that they cannot be considered unusual, and they will cost you points."

"It's still subjective," came the same voice from the audience.

"Yes," Giles admitted, "wit, humor, charm, cleverness, originality, complexity—all these are subjective. But our judges are respected editors. Their selections, their emendations and, yes, their contributions to the puzzles of others have given us all pleasure for many years. All contestants have, properly, agreed to accept their decision as final and binding."

"Is there a time limit, Mr. Sullivan?" one of the contestants asked.

"We must be finished by eight o'clock, to allow the waiters to set up the tables for the dinner, which will commence promptly at nine. The judges need sufficient time to do their jobs well. This isn't as easy as the solvers contest by a long shot. The speeches and awards will start promptly at ten-thirty, and we will be out of here well before midnight. Is everyone ready?"

"Yes!" came the enthusiastic roar.

"Then when I give the signal, you may turn over your sheets. Printed or handwritten references are permitted, but I warn you, the time spent researching will almost guarantee finishing late. The theme is *Weapons*. Go!"

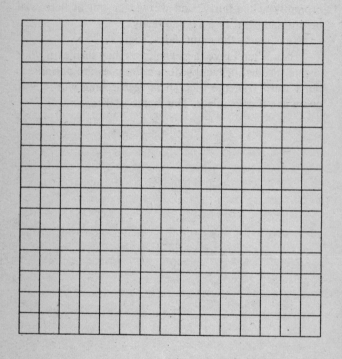

❖❖❖❖❖❖❖❖❖❖❖❖❖❖ 31 ❖❖❖❖

"HERE YOU ARE, GILES"—ISABEL PUT THE COPIES IN front of him—"all six, hot off the press."

"In what order did they finish?"

"Kantor first, Miklosz thirty seconds behind. Third was a"—she consulted her list—"a Thomas Engelberg; you know him?"

"A nice young man, a real comer. He made the first twenty last year. How about the rest of the suspects?"

"You're not interested in anyone but our directors, are you?"

"Not in the slightest, just those six."

"Delmore Rankin came in seventh, almost ten minutes behind Janos. Vergil Yount was twelfth, about five minutes after Delmore. Caroline was sixteenth, and Lila limped home in forty-eighth position. But that isn't necessarily the order of prizes, is it?"

"With times as close as the first ten have, other criteria will probably become the deciding factors. Also, if anyone made a mistake, a nonexistent word or an illegal or false clue, that would put him out of the running immediately. But it's clear that only Norbert and Janos, and possibly Delmore, have a chance at a prize."

"I made a set for myself, too, Giles. Let's work independently and compare notes later."

"You haven't had much experience with crosswords, Isabel, and you've never constructed a puzzle."

"I'm a quick study, Sullivan, and I've had lots of experience catching copying, plagiarism, faking grades, and all the other tricks the little monsters can think up to plague a teacher with. This can't be very different, so shut up and deal."

After five minutes Isabel said, "I've got it," and looked up. Giles was staring down at the table, his face pale.

"You knew which one to look at, didn't you?"

"Yes. And it was there."

"I found it almost right away. It's a great puzzle but—certain things stand out. Did you see where he had 'poison'?—I'm sure a police lab could prove this by the disturbance of the paper fibers—and he erased it and made it 'poised'? Why should anyone throw away a good theme word of six letters, unless he was trying to hide?"

"That's precisely what he was trying to do, consciously or unconsciously. And I'm sure, had he not been near the end of the puzzle, and fatigued, and worried about the competition, he would have realized it was not a wise thing to do. Not only did he lose a theme word and six theme letters; look at what he had to do at sixty-eight Across and seventy-one Across to complete the construction. He had two perfectly good words there, had he kept poison, and instead he used two perfectly terrible words. Take a look in the reference books. Are they there?" Isabel checked, and nodded her head. "Even so, if I were a judge, I would penalize him for those words."

"He missed another theme word, Giles, by not using poison. At sixty-eight Across."

"But that's not a weapon."

"Depends on who plays it, Giles."

"Don't be funny, Isabel. This is serious. Did you notice all the other directors had either poison or cyanide. One of them had both, but he had neither. It was natural for at least one of those words to be on their minds, but to him they spelled danger."

"That was the first thing that caught my attention."

"And the weapons he chose, Isabel. None of the others had even *one* of them; he had *three* in that category. They must have been burning in his mind. He could no more help putting them down than he could help breathing. To the others these were not weapons; to him they were, since he had already used one of that type to kill Brundage."

"Couldn't he have changed at least these? They were absolute giveaways."

"You haven't ever constructed a puzzle, Isabel, or you wouldn't have asked. After a certain number of words have been filled in, you can't make any major changes. Everything interlocks. You might as well throw the puzzle away and start fresh. One or two letters, such as the poison—poised pair, that's possible. Whole words? Never."

"Why didn't he lose the contest, then? Anything would be better than this."

"Losing the contest, not winning the prize, meant losing everything for him. He *had* to get the money. With the money he stood a chance; without the money he was dead."

"Then why did he bother to change *poison*? If he didn't care whether or not he was discovered, he could have left it."

"He did care, obviously. But when he got deeper into the construction, he realized that the money was more important than my accusation, and since he couldn't avoid

163

the words he used for weapons, he figured he might as well go full out to win."

"What a mind, to come up with this under these conditions."

"You have no idea, Isabel. Can you imagine the pressure he was under? The speed with which he had to work? His whole life riding on the piece of paper he was working on? Can you imagine the power of that magnificent mind, the drive to survive, the need to win, the desire to show his brilliance struggling against the imperative not to reveal that he is the killer? And with it all, the beauty of his composition, the cleverness of his clues? What a waste. What a pity."

"Is he sure to win?"

"If I were a judge, I'd vote for him."

"If you were a judge, you'd put him in jail."

"I'd have to, Isabel. The law must be upheld."

"Aside from the ethical problem—I know you sympathize with him and would really like to help him—if he isn't arrested and charged, five others will die in his place for all practical purposes."

"The problem is, Isabel, a crossword isn't evidence. There really isn't any way to use it to convict him or even to indict him."

"I wish I could help, darling, but this is outside my field. Do you want me to call Henry Winston?"

Giles smiled ruefully. "I'm the guy *he* consults on criminal matters."

"Nothing I can do to help?"

"Right now, darling, you're a distraction. Go into the bar and flirt with Cary Grant."

She kissed his cheek. "See you in an hour, darling."

32

ISABEL PUT DOWN HER COFFEE CUP AND TURNED TO HER right. "It's almost time for the awards," she said. "You *will* watch over Giles, won't you? You promised."

"The only way I could get closer to him," Percival said, "is if you and I changed seats, although it would serve him right if he got his head banged in, just once." Percival rubbed his big right fist, leaving no doubt as to who should do the banging in.

"Changing seats would just make him suspicious," Isabel said. "I don't want him even to know I asked you. Did you get Lieutenant Faber?"

"He's got a man at every exit and he's here himself, in the back someplace, where he can see everything."

"They're not, uh, conspicuous, are they?"

"In my book, anybody wearing a monkey suit is conspicuous. Are you going to tell me what's going on?"

"I don't know myself what Giles is going to do. I just don't want him hurt."

Giles stood up and tapped the lectern with his cane. "May I have your attention, please. Those of you who have not yet finished your coffee, please do so at once.

The award ceremony is about to begin, and I will tolerate no clinking china or gulping noises during the presentations. Thank you.

"We have an exceptionally large number of contestants for this, our fiftieth-anniversary celebration contests. Although these contests were limited to members of the Cruciverbal Club, the list includes some of the most accomplished and skillful puzzlers in the country. The winners in each category can indeed be proud, and even those who did not win can remember this event as one of the highlights of cruciverbalism."

Giles turned to the wings and signaled for the envelopes to be delivered. He turned back to the microphone. "We will announce the winners of the solvers contest first. Engraved plaques and the prize checks—for which we thank the publishing houses whose contributions made this possible—will be given to each of the six winners by our esteemed manager, Mr. Arthur Fredericks — stand up, Arthur—on my right, as soon as each one makes his short, repeat *short*, acceptance speech."

There was dead silence as Giles opened the first envelope. "Ah, the winner of the third prize of five thousand dollars in the solvers contest is—Lester Stewart." There was a burst of applause. A tall young man got up and started walking toward the dais. Giles stopped him at the foot of the dais with an open palm. "One moment, please, Lester; I want to tell the audience and the press a little about you."

"Lester Stewart," Giles said, "has been a member for ten years. In the last five years he has placed in the top twenty in both the solvers and the constructors contests. We knew that sooner or later Lester would break into the winner's circle, but none of us, I think, expected it to happen this year. We're all very proud of you, Lester, and we hope and expect that you'll hit a first prize next time out."

Lester walked up to the microphone and said, "Thank you, Mr. Sullivan. I really appreciate the honor and the check, and I'll keep practicing. Thank you all again." He shook Giles's hand and walked back to where Arthur Fredericks handed him the plaque and the check. There was more applause and a shout of "Way to go, Lester" as he resumed his seat.

Giles opened the second envelope. "And the winner of the second prize of ten thousand dollars is—Janos Miklosz, one of our best puzzlers and the popular and efficient chairman of our board of directors." Giles turned left and said, "Stand at your place for a minute, Janny. I want to say a few words."

"Janos Miklosz," Giles said, "was born in Hungary and lived there for his first eighteen years. He spoke a language that has no resemblance to Greek, Latin, or Germanic, the core roots of English. He escaped to Brazil, where for several years he spoke Portuguese and Spanish. When he arrived in New York, he had only bare conversational and business English. With his usual drive and intensity, within one year Janos was fluent in English and had joined the Cruciverbal Club. Two years later, in the first contest he entered, he placed in the top one hundred, a feat many native-born Americans have never accomplished. Come to the mike now, Janos, old friend, and tell the audience how you did it."

The applause was loud and long as Janos walked the few steps to the lectern. "In spite of the way Giles made it sound," Janos said, "it's an advantage to be born a Hungarian, for crosswords at least. There is no way you can communicate with anyone else in the world, even partially, except possibly some Finns. A Hungarian is forced, absolutely forced, to become a linguist, since every root in English is completely foreign to him. Every word, every bit of grammar, is approached freshly, without misconception."

"So it is your advice, then," Giles said, "if we want to improve our verbal skills, that we all move to Hungary for a year?"

"It is my *hope*," Janos said, "that *all* Hungarians can come to this beautiful land of freedom and live here forever. Thank you." He shook Giles's hand and marched over to Arthur Fredericks to collect his plaque and his check.

Giles held up the last envelope. "This is the big one, ladies and gentlemen, the first prize of twenty-five thousand dollars. I'll open the envelope, but we all know who it must be—yes, it's our own speed queen, Mrs. Lila Quinn." The applause and cheers resounded through the room, bouncing off the hard-surfaced walls and carved plaster ceiling. Giles motioned Lila to stand up, and applauded her himself. After a full minute, he turned back to the microphone. "Although Lila Quinn is legally a senior citizen, she is quite a doddering senescent—that's two nine-letter words—as anyone who has been stabbed by her sharp tongue can tell you. Lila, will you come here and say a few words? Polite ones, please?"

Lila walked slowly to the lectern. "Polite ones? Okay. I'll do it for you, Giles, but it will spoil my day. Thank you, ladies and gentlemen, from the bottom of my heart. I've been praying for a first ever since I joined the club and this year, thank God, I got my wish. I leave you with one thought: You're never too old."

"For those few who don't know about Lila," Giles said, "she is the undisputed blitz-Scrabble champion of New York, and possibly the universe and the outlying districts. She has been a member of the club for ten years, and her unorthodox puzzle-solving techniques have been the bafflement and frustration of everyone who has come up against her. Do you have a word of advice for our members, Lila?"

"Sure. Don't try to do it my way; do it the right way. Thank you."

"Thank you, Lila. And now the high point of the evening, the peak of achievement, the constructors contest. Difficult as it is to win a prize in the solvers contest, it is ten times as hard to show in the constructors contest. Our judges had a hard time deciding the placement of the first three, so good were all the top contestants, but they finally made their selections. For those of you who want to know how you placed, the ranking for this contest as well as for the first contest will be posted on the bulletin board.

"There were more than four hundred entrants in the solvers contest and over one hundred in the constructors contest, so anyone who got into the top fifty of the first contest, or into the top twenty of the second, can feel very, very proud indeed. Anyone who achieved both can truly consider himself of master rank.

"And now we come to the awards for the constructors contest. Third prize, five thousand dollars, and the winner is—Thomas Engelberg." A short, chubby young man at the right side of the room stood up. "Remain standing at your seat for a moment, Tommy; I'm going to tell everyone about you. Thomas has been a member of the club for only three years, but in that short time he has made his mark here. In his first year, Tommy was in the top twenty in *both* categories, and he has been near the top in every contest since then. Tommy is our most promising puzzler—can you imagine what he'll be like when he's thirty?—and we're looking forward to the day when he has time to *really* practice. Tommy, our youngest active member, is studying medicine with a view toward specializing in psychiatry. I'm sure he'll find a fertile source of practice in the crossword game. Please come up to the lectern, Tommy, and say a few words to your admirers."

"Thank you for your kind words, Mr. Sullivan. I love those words, as I have always loved words. I hope to be worthy of your praise and I will do my best to fulfill your prophecy. And I sure can use the money. Thank you again."

Cheers and applause followed Tommy's steps all the way back to his table. A bottle of champagne had been ordered by his friends while he was on the dais, and the proceedings were halted while all those at his table raised their glasses in his honor.

When all was quiet again, Giles tore open the next envelope. "Our second-prize winner is"—Giles turned to his left—"Dr. Norbert Kantor. Stand up, Norbert, while I embarrass you a little." The applause swelled as Kantor nodded right and left, acknowledging his achievement and popularity.

"Dr. Kantor"—Giles had to speak above the applause—"Dr. Kantor is Professor of Philology at New York's most prestigious university, the author of six highly regarded books and of innumerable papers. His work has been called seminal and has provided a completely new way of studying verbal communication, hinting at the genetic coding which he believes controls the structure of all human communication by symbols. He is a world authority in his field and is generally recognized as one of the greatest intellects of our generation. With all this, he is an officer of his temple and deeply involved in charitable work. Norbert has been a director of the club for two years and has given of his time and energy without stint. Were it not for his propensity for inflicting bad puns on his fellow members, he would be one of the most popular fellows in the club. Please come to the microphone, Norbert, and say a very few words."

"Thank you, Giles, ladies and gentlemen. I am honored and pleased to be awarded this prize and, like Tommy, I can use the money. This contest, and the attendant publicity, should call the attention of the whole country to the importance of words as a medium of communication, particularly considering the encroachment of multisensorial media such as television. I have long felt that the use of words—'In the beginning was the Word'—was the first manifestation of civilization. If our work, or play—crosswords are both—advances the love of words even a little, we will have done more for humanity than all the politicians and armies together. Thank you."

There was even more applause as Kantor picked up his plaque and his check and returned to his seat on the dais. As he sat down Janos shook his hand strongly.

Giles held up the last envelope. In a few seconds the crowd fell silent. "I am not going to open this envelope yet," Giles said. "We have another surprise for you, another first." He turned toward the wings. Two young men rolled out a small table on which stood an opaque projector. They pulled down the large movie screen at the wall behind the dais, plugged the projector into an outlet, focused the lens on the blank screen, and shut the projector off again.

171

"Tonight," Giles announced, "we are going to project, for your amazement and your pleasure"—he rolled his *r*'s and his voice took on a ringmaster's exaggerated tone—"the winning construction, and will describe how it came about. I think you will agree that it is one of the most unusual and possibly the greatest crossword you have ever seen, and, considering the conditions under which it was made, a feat of superhuman achievement. And as an added divertissement, I will tell you a mystery story. Will someone lower the lights, please, just enough to be in keeping with the story."

"What's he trying to pull?" Percival whispered.

"I don't know," Isabel whispered back, "but this has to be it. Keep your eyes on Giles and get ready to do whatever has to be done."

In the half-darkness, Oliver slowly shifted his position closer to the back of Isabel's chair. In the rear of the ballroom Lieutenant Faber whispered into his walkie-talkie.

Giles stood at the lectern, outlined by the dim reading light. "Last Wednesday," Giles said softly, "the directors of the Cruciverbal Club met at my home for the final preparations for this contest weekend. We were dining before the meeting. After the appetizer and soup, the entree was served. Two minutes later, Harvey Brundage was dead. Murdered. Someone had fed him, or placed into his food, a capsule of potassium cyanide.

"Though not the most popular member of this club, Harvey Brundage was a guest in my house and therefore under my protection. The dish that killed him was served by my staff. I was seated on his right at the round table. Miss Isabel Macintosh, my houseguest and a dear friend, was seated on his left. On Miss Macintosh's left sat Janos

Miklosz, then Delmore Rankin and Caroline Trimble. On my right was Vergil Yount, then Norbert Kantor, and Lila Quinn. It would have been easy for me or for Miss Macintosh to place poison in Harvey's plate, and impossible for any of the other directors to do so without being seen. Everyone agreed that no one had reached toward or made any kind of motion toward Harvey or his plate. The room was brightly lit, as was the table.

"I present this to you as a problem—no, a puzzle. All good cruciverbalists love a puzzle. Here is one that has frustrated a good many people for the past four days. It is clear that one of the eight of us murdered Harvey Brundage. But which one?

"Since I had elected myself detective-in-charge, I eliminated myself and Miss Macintosh. I was sure that the butler didn't do it, nor had the cook. The suspects were, in my mind at least, much as it pains me to say it, the six remaining directors of the club, the ones seated on the dais to my left."

Giles paused and took a drink of water. He pulled a sheet of paper from his breast pocket and unfolded it. "Here is a copy of the most interesting construction to come out of today's contest. The name of the constructor has been blanked out. The judges have kindly—some of the clues are pretty far out—added a few words of clarification for some of the more esoteric clues."

"If you're having trouble, Giles," came a voice from the audience, "I could rent you my nine-year-old son."

"We have here," Giles smiled, "among the press and our distinguished guests, some people, hard as it may be to believe, who have not devoted every waking moment to crosswords."

Giles placed the completed puzzle on the base of the

ACROSS

1 William Tell often took ___
5 Fish in the barbershop quartet
9 Alabama woman
14 Derek—look!
15 Top—morning connection
16 Topless tents
17 Role for Red
18 What a violent bartender may do
20 Over the waves
22 Say for sure
23 Dogcatcher's profit
24 Whose fault is this?
26 Gifted person?
29 It's all a put-on
32 Volsungasaga king
33 Hoopla
34 Map 11.
35 Re money, he's where it's at
39 Trunks that aren't 29 Across
41 Golfer's shoe
42 Have ___ the ears
45 Tooth of a type
47 7% of land: Abbr.
48 "I cannot tell ___"
49 This has a-way with a song
51 Novel subtitled *Virtue Rewarded*
53 McGarrett's aide
54 Jose or Pedro
55 Tars' bars
57 Tired partner
60 Vegetable hunter
64 Did a ditty
66 Really hip joints
67 Piano piece
68 Oil-yielding tree of Central America
69 It's kept peeled
70 Once, once
71 Chief of Malayan Moro tribe

DOWN

1 Beginner's network
2 A tennis shot returned
3 Chihuahua cheers
4 60% of women get their legislation
5 Belinsky and Diddley
6 Opp. of Pac.-Pac.'s?
7 Shake unhesitatingly
8 Gambia's only neighbor
9 Parisian's, palindromically
10 Williams player
11 Big *gatto*
12 Maid's concern
13 Short helper
19 Acceptable, to Augustus
21 Broadcast and ransack
25 D.C. agent served dinner
27 Spooner's fluorescent rolls
28 Incisiveness
29 Courtroom writeup
30 Figurehead's position
31 Firestarter
36 Inventor's basis
37 End of Annie's song
38 Square
40 Play tricks successfully
43 Bag End resident
44 Historic leader
45 Chewed food solidifies
46 Almost a gem
50 Composed
51 ∕ ⌄ ⌄ ⌄
52 Have ___ to grind
54 Pet grp.
56 Ripley's middle
58 Camaguey's home
59 Puzzle with no sound?
61 2¢
62 Tee tail
65 Wash. magazine

CONSTRUCTORS CONTEST

opaque projector and snapped on the light. The puzzle jumped into visibility on the screen. Giles adjusted the fine focus until every letter, every clue, was perfectly sharp, then shut off the projector again.

Satisfied that all was ready, Giles returned to the lectern. "You may remember," Giles said, "that the theme of the solvers puzzle was *Missiles* and the theme of the constructors puzzle was *Weapons*. This was not an accidental choice. I had the constructor of the contest puzzles—yes, Hannibal—revise his work on very short notice and put into the solvers puzzle two words, *pellet*, and *beebee*—and one other word I will discuss later—which would have meaning only to the murderer. This made the killer even more nervous than he would normally be, causing him even more stress than he was already suffering. He did not know whether or not I knew how Brundage was killed and who had done it, or if these two dangerous words had appeared in the puzzle by accident. So the killer did not know, could not be sure, what action to take.

"Then when the constructors puzzle theme was announced, *Weapons*, he knew I knew, but what could he do? Walk out? Do a poor job? Anything he was in a position to do was tantamount to a confession. Once the police knew who he was and how the murder had been committed, he was lost. Had he *really* disposed of all the evidence? Had *no one* observed any suspicious actions? Was there *really* no way to follow his trail? The police have a great many facilities; they are very persistent, very thorough when they are sure they have the guilty party.

"If he was lucky," Giles continued, "if the words in the solvers puzzle meant nothing, then he could take the money and run. If I knew—for who else could have told Hannibal what to do?—how it was done and who the killer was, he was already lost. So he took the proper odds; he did his best, and a very good job it was too."

Giles walked over to the projector, asked that all the lights be turned off, and snapped on the projector. The magnified puzzle and its clues flashed on the screen, the glow from the projector outlining Sullivan's body.

"I'll kill him," Percival whispered. "He knew all the time, didn't he?"

"Knowing isn't proving," Isabel whispered. "I still don't see how he's going to do it. And you don't know it, but Giles has five other problems to juggle at the same time. I hope he doesn't drop the ball."

Standing in front of the screen holding the microphone in his left hand, Giles began lecturing in a dry, scholarly voice. "Most people think of missiles as high-technology self-propelled explosive devices. But there are other types of missiles, not just ballistic missiles and cruise missiles, but arrows, spears, darts, pellets, beebees, all sorts of projectiles. The same is true of weapons."

For a moment the audience was quiet, then there was a hissing of whispers. The whispering became murmuring, the murmurs grew more numerous, louder, until, it seemed, everyone was talking. "Look at fourteen Across," was clearly heard, then, "Did you see eighteen Across?" There was laughter, shouts of "Get that sixty Across," "Two Down," and "Twenty-seven Down," and "Forty-five Down," and half the room was pointing things out to the other half. Suddenly, spontaneously, the audience burst into applause. The applause grew louder and continued even more loudly as Giles tapped the floor with his cane. He had to hit the floor several times, harder each time, before the applause began to die down.

"Yes, ladies and gentlemen," Giles said, "a great puzzle. You can see why, although Norbert Kantor finished first, this construction was chosen for first prize. But there are other matters that must be discussed."

Using his cane as a pointer, Giles touched a word on the screen. "Here is an interesting clue. Not a clue in the crossword sense, but in the solving-a-crime sense. The word *poised*. Why isn't it *poison*? To change two letters would have been simple; why didn't he? It would have given him two good words as crossings instead of two obscure words, bad words. As a matter of fact, he *did* change the word. If you look closely, you can see that it was once *poison* and then erased, changed to poised. There are techniques for seeing what the disturbed paper fibers once held; they used to use iodine vapor, now there are better ways. I leave that to the police. But think of this; why would anyone in the middle of a contest, where every second counted, throw away a theme word—poison is certainly a weapon—and six theme letters, and lose at least ten seconds, and have to dredge up out of his encyclopedic memory two very obscure words? Why? The answer is simple: He wanted to hide that, to him, poison was a weapon. The other five directors all had either 'poison' or 'cyanide' in their puzzles; one even had both words. Why not? It was on their minds and they all had clear consciences."

"Then look at these words: 'AIR RIFLE,' 'PEA-SHOOTER,' and 'BLOWGUNS.' None of the contestants, and I don't mean just the directors, had a single one of these words or similar words. To them, these simply were not weapons. This puzzle had *three*. Why? Because to this constructor they were all weapons, because he had used an air-propelled pellet, a blowgun, a peashooter of sorts, to kill Harvey Brundage."

A burst of whispers came from the audience, a buzzing as of a beehive disturbed. To Giles's left, the directors looked at one another, worried, questioning. Only Lila Quinn kept her eyes fixed straight ahead of her.

Giles turned off the projector and walked back to the lectern. The reading light emphasized every line in his tired face. In a quiet, almost conversational tone of voice Giles said, "Where is the long ivory cigarette holder, Janny? The one you used to blow the cyanide *capsule* into Harvey Brundage's mashed potatoes?"

The audience exploded, questions asked and questions answered. Louder and louder. Heads together at a table, then a turning to other tables. Eyes, heads, one by one slowly focused on the director's side of the dais.

Lila Quinn reached her left hand out protectively and rested it on Janos Miklosz's right arm. Delmore Rankin got up to stand at Miklosz's left side and to put his right hand lightly on Miklosz's left shoulder. Norbert Kantor stared at his old friend, his face full of compassion. Vergil refilled his wineglass and, about to drink it down, changed his mind and pushed it past Lila to Miklosz. Caroline Trimble began crying softly.

Giles held his hand up for silence; the noise began to die down. Finally the audience was hushed. Without moving from his chair Janos Miklosz said, "My cigarette holder? I gave up smoking, Giles, a while ago. I threw the holder away. It's probably in a garbage dump now."

"Why not confess, Janny? You can save five people, five good people. It would be the honorable way."

"Confess to what, Giles? Conjecture? If you have evidence, produce it. If not, let's finish the ceremony."

Giles looked weary. He stood for a moment, head down, then spoke. "To all the news people here, please announce in your newspapers that I have found the killer of Harvey

Brundage, that I accuse Janos Miklosz of murdering Harvey Brundage. You need not say that the police are satisfied or that the D.A. is ready to ask for an indictment, just that I have found the murderer. This is important. I will put my accusation in writing for all the reporters and will repeat it in front of the TV cameras. I will take all responsibility for any lawsuits, although I think there is little danger of that. And Miklosz is right. We must complete the ceremony to the end, to the bitter end."

"Is Giles crazy?" Percival whispered. "I could take him down right now and in one night, guaranteed, in one night he'd be *begging* me to let him confess."

"You're not a policeman now," Isabel whispered back. "Giles has to have something in mind. Let him ride."

"What mind? He's got the killer; close the case."

"If you don't shut up," Isabel said, "you'll be picking steak knives out of your fat belly for a week."

Giles said formally, "Ladies and gentlemen, you have had demonstrated to you this evening one of the greatest exhibitions of cruciverbalism the world had ever seen or may ever see again. Mr. Miklosz's victory tonight is unprecedented in the history of the club. We have had two other occasions since the club was founded, fifty years ago, when a single person won prizes in both categories. Once, two third prizes were won; once a third and a second. No one has ever won a first and a second and, if it hadn't been for Lila Quinn's extraordinary talent, Janos Miklosz would have won two firsts. When you get a chance, study the winning construction. Notice the unusual words I mentioned before, and others even more unusual. Note what a high percentage of the total letters were in theme words, and in this, you really should count *poison*. Be amazed at the huge number of theme words used. And most important, look at the beauty, the wit, the humor, of the clues. And when you marvel at their cleverness, their complexity, and their fairness, realize, too, the time pressure, that this was done during a contest. If for nothing else, we should honor this puzzle; it will be posted, framed, on the wall of this club forever, for the greatest set of clues I have ever seen in my life. Realize, too, that Janos Miklosz was not just under time pressure, but under the pressure of the crime he had committed, and other pressures which cannot be discussed at this time. You have been privileged, ladies and gentlemen, to have witnessed a demonstration by one of the most powerful verbally oriented minds of all times."

Giles took a deep breath. "Now," he said, "it is time to bring the ceremony to a close, to award the final prize. As is customary, I will tell you a little more about our great puzzler.

"Janos came by his great talents naturally. His father was a respected educator and his mother was—"

"No, no," Janos whispered urgently from his seat down the table. "No more, Giles, please."

"Janos," Giles said, smiling, "is modest about his achievements and background. In my function as master of ceremonies I boned up on the backgrounds of those people I felt were most likely to win prizes. In Janny's case I could get very little, and he was so shy that I had to call on an old friend in Washington to trace the location and present names of this very self-effacing family."

"Don't, Giles," Janos said desperately. "It's dangerous."

"Janny doesn't want me to go on with this eulogy to his illustrious family. So shy is he that he changed his name when he came to the new world, and his family did the same when they scattered. But we were able to find out everything, and you will all be surprised when I reveal who—"

"*No!*" Janos screamed. "*No!*" He grabbed a knife from the table and dived toward Giles. Instinctively Giles twisted the shaft of his cane and lifted the point of the sword just enough so that Janos Miklosz's plunging body impaled itself on the sharp shining silver blade.

JANNY'S FACE CONTORTED IN SHOCK. HIS HANDS SPRANG open; the knife clattered to the floor. Janny fell forward, hands clawing at Giles's lapels. "Don't," Janny begged. "Don't tell. . . ."

Giles grabbed Janny around the shoulders with his left arm, his right hand desperately trying to keep the saber from moving, from ripping any more of Janny's lung.

"My mother . . ." Janny pleaded, sagging against Giles. They'll kill . . ."

Percival grabbed the back of Janos's pants with his huge left hand and held the wounded man erect. He put his right arm firmly around Giles's waist to steady him. "Miklosz," Percival said into Janny's ear, "where's the rest of the cyanide?"

"Gone," Miklosz whispered. "All gone."

"And the capsules?" Percival raised his voice. "Where's the rest of the box of capsules?"

"No more." Miklosz's voice was weaker.

"The paint?" Percival growled. "You painted the capsule to look like an almond."

"Threw out." Janos's voice was barely audible.

"The brush!" Percival roared into his ear. "The one you used to paint the capsule."

"By the stencils." Janos breathed out softly and closed his eyes.

Percival let Janos down gently to the floor. He placed the unconscious man on his side carefully, so that the sword would not move. Giles followed him down, holding the handle of the sword in place. "Get a doctor," Percival told the breathless Lieutenant Faber, who had just reached the dais. "And get a man over to the Miklosz office quick. Get the brush from the drawer where the labeling stencils are, wherever that is, and get it to the lab. There have to be tiny bits of paint in the base of the bristles."

"He probably cleaned it good," Faber said.

"Of course he cleaned it." Percival took Faber by the arm and led him aside. "The guy's a brain. But your man will *find* tiny bits of paint at the base of the bristles. Right?" Percival stared at Faber intently. "He killed Brundage, didn't he?"

Faber stared back, nodded, and said, "Right, chief."

Percival stepped back to the fallen Janos. He looked down at Giles, still kneeling at Janny's side. "Good work, Giles," Percival said.

Giles, tears streaming down his face, looked up at his brother.

"I'm proud of you," Percival said.

 34

"**D**ON'T TRY ANYTHING FUNNY," PERCIVAL SAID, TAK-ing the glass of Jameson's from Oliver's tray. "I cashed in an awful lot of credit cards to get you straight home, and I don't want to look like a jerk."

"Mr. Yount's friend was influential in this too," Oliver said. "And Mr. Giles has friends who were also very helpful."

"It never hurts to have friends in Washington," Percival agreed, "but it's the local connections that close the deal."

"It was self-defense," Caroline whispered, her eyes still red.

"Giles was carrying a concealed weapon, Miss Trimble," Percival pointed out. "He'll still have to show up in the morning, but I've got it all set. There won't even be a memo in the files."

"Did you think he was really trying to kill you?" Delmore asked.

"I believe he would have given his life to protect his mother," Giles said. "So *my* life was an unimportant consideration."

"Would you really have revealed his mother's name

and address?" Norbert asked. "Knowing it would condemn her to death?"

"I don't know what I would have done," Giles replied. "You may have noticed how I was dragging things out."

"If Giles hadn't gotten Janos to expose himself as the killer," Isabel said, "by Wednesday all five of you would have had your lives destroyed."

"Janos didn't expose himself as the killer," Lila said. "He exposed himself as a man trying to protect his mother."

"There was no way to *prove* Janos was the killer," Vergil said. "All he had to do was sit tight, collect his prizes, and run."

"We know from his puzzle that he had to be the murderer," Isabel said. "The police would have found some traces when they dug."

"That's a long way from an indictment," Percival said, "much less a conviction. I was the guy who got the evidence out of him."

"You never mentioned, Giles, how you figured it out," Delmore said.

"It was Saturday morning. Isabel was having an ice cream soda. She blew the paper wrapper off the straw, the way kids do, and hit me on the nose. Then the flash came. Janos had the capsule in his empty cigarette holder. It was painted the color of a sliver of toasted almond. Right, Percival?"

Percival nodded. "That was one of the things we were holding back."

"When everyone's attention was on the serving of the trout," Giles said, "Janos blew—it was like a little blowgun—blew the capsule into Harvey's plate. Probably into the mashed potatoes, so it wouldn't bounce out."

"On Saturday morning," Lila said, "we were still trying to figure out step one. By Saturday night we had a brand-new contest puzzle with special words in it. Giles was very lucky he was able to reach Hannibal so fast. I mean, the guy could have been out on his yacht or something."

"That *was* lucky," Isabel said.

"And then Hannibal dropped everything to make a new puzzle for Giles? They must be real close friends."

"Giles has known him for many years."

"That's what I figured," Lila said complacently.

"I'd like to get back to the ethics of what happened," Norbert said. "Harvey was murdered. That's an illegal act and against the Commandments. But *he* was trying to commit an unethical act, to win the prizes by blackmail, and he would have destroyed the six of us if we didn't accede to his plan, which was an immoral act. There was no way to bring the murderer to justice—although we were all pleased that Harvey was no longer with us—and no way to punish him under the law. So you, Giles, decided to blackmail the murderer by threatening the death of an innocent person, his mother, to *force* the murderer to commit an illegal act, that is, to try to kill you in order to save the life of his mother, which is, in itself, a noble act. How do you reconcile all this, Giles?"

"I don't. I just decided that the five of you outweighed the one of him, especially since he was a murderer. I also found out from my friend in Washington that Janos was not just smuggling eight-bit computer chips, but also sixteen-bit chips and even some stolen thirty-two-bit chips, the kind that can be used for weapons as well as for computers."

"But Janos was *forced* into smuggling," Caroline said. "To protect his mother. Just as—other people were forced to do things they wouldn't normally do."

"If in order to save his child's life a man takes *your* child's life, is that a moral act?" Norbert asked. "No, you can always find reasons for any action, no matter how evil. The only way to live is to follow the basic rules for humanity, the Ten Commandments."

"I stabbed him in self-defense, Norbert. The Ten Commandments allow that."

"You *provoked* him into attacking you and then you stabbed him," Norbert said. "How do you feel about that?"

"Bad, Norbert. Really bad. But I didn't intend to injure him. All I wanted was for him to admit he was the killer, so the papers would print it and you five would be saved. He never would have been convicted. I'm a lawyer; I know."

"You came within an inch of killing him." Norbert wouldn't let it die. "Janny is still on the critical list."

"He was coming at me with a knife. I had the cane in my hands. It was instinctive. I didn't even try. . . . All the years of training . . . In fencing, you form a mental image of where the heart is. The point goes there almost by itself. There was no time to think, like blinking when someone swings at you. Only at the last moment was I able to drop the point."

"The next time," Percival said, "you read about a cop faced with a killer in an alley and the killer has a knife and the cop pulls his gun, the next time maybe you'll understand a little better when the cop pulls the trigger. If you had been a cop, Giles, right now you'd be up on charges and there'd be nothing I could do to help you. You'd have a hell of a time proving you knew he was trying to kill you, and a hell of a time proving there was no better way to subdue him. And if I was sitting in judgment on you, Giles, you'd never convince me you didn't provoke him deliberately."

"The police, Percival, as officers of the state, have such

powers that it is important to put more restraints on them than on ordinary citizens."

"Was there no other way, Giles?" Norbert asked. "Couldn't you have approached him and threatened to reveal his mother's name and address unless he confessed?"

"I thought of that, Norbert, but it wouldn't have worked. Given time to think, he would have realized it was an empty threat and that after he collected the prizes and disappeared, you five would have been the only victims."

"What will happen to Janny's prize money?" Delmore asked.

"It's his," Isabel said. "He earned it, every penny. It must go to him. Or to his heirs," she added grimly.

"His sister?" Lila asked. "They'll just take it away from her after they frame her as a spy."

"Between Vergil's friends in Washington and Giles's friend, I am sure a way can be found to get the money to Janny's Hungarian refugee friends. They'll know how to get Janny's mother out. Which is what the money was for in the first place."

"If Janny doesn't make it," Vergil said, "I will see to it personally."

"It's very late," Isabel said. "Giles has been through a terrible ordeal. Your Talmudic analysis, Norbert, is very interesting, but at two A.M., I can't handle it. After you finish your coffee, Oliver will arrange cabs for everyone."

Lila was the last to leave. She paused at the door. "It's not good to be alone," she told Isabel.

"It has its compensations," Isabel said. "Peace. Quiet."

"That I've had for ten years, Isabel; believe me, they're overrated. Peace and quiet are not the only good things in life. Bad as this was"—her hand made a wide circle to encompass the past week—"bad as it was, it's the most interesting thing that ever happened to me."

"Crosswords and blitz-Scrabble are no longer enough for you?"

"It's a living," Lila admitted. "But this . . . The same kind of thinking goes into it—the same deduction, the same intuition. The description of the words in crosswords are even called clues. So alike in so many ways. Maybe that's why . . . I wouldn't admit this to anyone else, Isabel, but in spite of all my troubles, I enjoyed the adventure."

❖❖❖❖❖❖❖❖❖❖❖❖❖❖❖❖❖❖❖❖❖❖❖❖ 35 ❖❖❖❖

Isabel came back to find Giles in the same position on the couch, head back, staring at the ceiling.

He didn't move for a while, then he sat up straight, decisively. "I'm going to defend Janny," he said.

"That's what I figured; what took you so long?"

"I'm going to get him off too," Giles insisted.

"Of course, Giles; you're the best."

"No fee." He looked at her sharply.

"Naturally." Satisfied, he stood up. She took his hand and led him to the stairs. "Percival was right," she said. "You would have made a lousy cop."

ILLEGAL

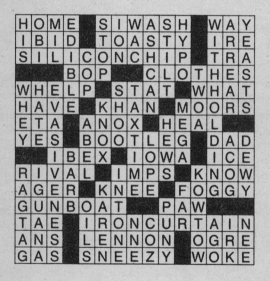

```
H O M E   S I W A S H   W A Y
I B I D   T O A S T Y   I R E
S I L I C O N C H I P   T R A
    B O P     C L O T H E S
W H E L P   S T A T   W H A T
H A V E   K H A N   M O O R S
E T A   A N O X   H E A L
Y E S   B O O T L E G   D A D
    I B E X   I O W A   I C E
R I V A L   I M P S   K N O W
A G E R   K N E E   F O G G Y
G U N B O A T     P A W
T A E   I R O N C U R T A I N
A N S   L E N N O N   O G R E
G A S   S N E E Z Y   W O K E
```

UNETHICAL

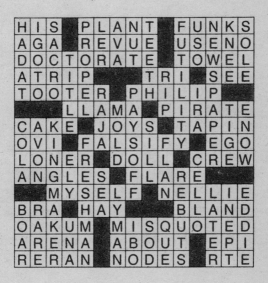

IMMORAL

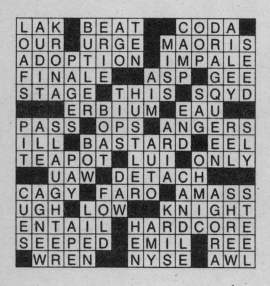

SOLVERS CONTEST—WINNING PUZZLE

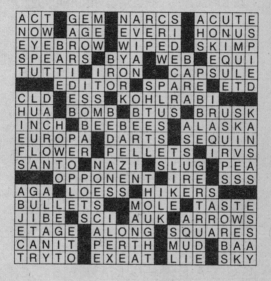

CONSTRUCTORS CONTEST—WINNING PUZZLE

ACROSS

1 William Tell often took ___   *A BOW

5 Fish in the barbershop   bass
    quartet

9 Alabama woman   Selma

14 Derek—look!   *Bolo (Bo + lo)

15 Top–morning connection   o' the

16 Topless tents   *EPEES (Tepees − t)

17 Role for Red   Clem (Skelton)

18 What a violent bartender may   *SLING SHOTS
    do

20 Over the waves   asea

22 Say for sure   aver

23 Dogcatcher's profit   net

24 Whose fault is this?   rift

26 Gifted person?   gabber

29 It's all a put-on   apparel

32 Volsungasaga king   Atli

33 Hoopla   cry

34 Map 11.   rds. (11. = lines)

35 Re money, he's where it's at   Laotian ("at" is a coin of Laos)

39 Trunks that aren't 29 Across   torsi

41 Golfer's shoe   wedge

42 Have ___ the ears   a wolf by (a cliché of ancient
                                         times [Bartlett's])

45 Tooth of a type   cog

47 7% of land: Abbr.   Eur.

48 "I cannot tell ___"   a lie

49 This has a-way with a song   Up, Up, and

51 Novel subtitled *Virtue*   Pamela
    Rewarded

53 McGarrett's aide   Dano (Hawaii Five-O)

54 Jose or Pedro   San

55 Tars' bars   brig

57 Tired partner   sick

60 Vegetable hunter   *PEA SHOOTER

64 Did a ditty   sung

66 Really hip joints   coxae

67 Piano piece   Nola

68 Oil-yielding tree of Central   eboe
    America

69 It's kept peeled   an eye   composite definition
                                       derived from *The Dell*
                                     Crossword Dictionary

70 Once, once   erst
71 Chief of Malayan Moro tribe   Dato

DOWN

1 Beginner's network   A B C
2 A tennis shot returned   *BOLA (a lob)
3 Chihuahua cheers   olés
4 60% of women get their   *WOMERA (women − en +
    legislation   E.R.A. ([alt. sp. of
                                       woomera, accdg. to
                                         *Scrabble Players
                                         Dictionary*])
5 Belinsky and Diddley   Bo's
6 Opp. of Pac.-Pac.'s?   *ATLATLS (Pacific, Atlantic)
7 Shake unhesitatingly   *SHIV (shiver-er)
8 Gambia's only neighbor   Senegal
9 Parisian's, palindromically   ses
10 Williams player   Eph
11 Big *gatto*   leone
12 Maid's concern   meter
13 Short helper   asst.
19 Acceptable, to Augustus   grata
21 Broadcast and ransack   *AIR RIFLE
25 D.C. agent served dinner   Fed
27 Spooner's fluorescent rolls   *BLOWGUNS (glow buns)
28 Incisiveness   bite
29 Courtroom writeup   acta
30 Figurehead's position   prow
31 Firestarter   pyro-
36 Inventor's basis   idea
37 End of Annie's song   *A GUN (You Can't Get a
                                         Man With a Gun)
38 Square   nerd
40 Play tricks successfully   slam (bridge)
43 Bag End resident   *BILBO (*Lord of the Rings*)
44 Historic leader   year one
45 Chewed food solidifies   *CUDGELS (cud, gels)
46 Almost a gem   opa (opal − 1)
50 Composed   poised
51 ˊ ˇ ˇ   paeon
52 Have ___ to grind   *AN AXE
54 Pet grp.   S.P.C.A.
56 Ripley's middle   it or
58 Camaguey's home   Cuba

59 Puzzle with no sound?   knot   ("not")
61 2¢   say   (opinion)
62 Tee tail   hee
65 Wash. magazine   Geo. (George Washington;
                                          GEO magazine)

Attention Mystery and Suspense Fans

Do you want to complete your collection of mystery and suspense stories by some of your favorite authors? Raymond Chandler, Erle Stanley Gardner, Ed McBain, Cornell Woolrich, among many others, and included in Ballantine's new Mystery Brochure.

For your FREE Mystery Brochure, fill in the coupon below and mail it to: